I FELL IN LOVE
WITH A
REAL STREET
THUG

Λ NOVEL BY

PEBBLES STARR

www.jadedpublications.com

TO BE NOTIFIED OF NEW RELEASES, CONTESTS, GIVEAWAYS,

AND BOOK SIGNINGS IN YOUR AREA, TEXT **BOOKS** TO **25827**

This novel is a work of fiction. Any reference to real people, events, establishments, or locales is intended only to give the fiction a sense of reality and authenticity. Other names, characters, and incidents occurring in the work are either the product of the author's imagination or are used fictitiously, as are those fictionalized events and events that involve real persons. Any character that happens to share the name of a person who is any acquaintance of the author, past or present, is purely coincidental and is in no way intended to be an actual account involving that person.

INSPIRED BY TRUE EVENTS

PROLOGUE
KHARI
2007

The beautiful set-up for my twin sister's baby shower made me briefly consider having one of my own. At 18, I was still a virgin who'd never put any serious thoughts into motherhood, yet something about the atmosphere gave me baby fever—not to mention the sight of everyone rubbing and fawning over Kylie's bulging belly. She was six months pregnant and gushing like she'd just been crowned Prom Queen.

Loving every moment of the coddling and complimentary gifts, Kylie greedily soaked up the attention as if it were her only source of nutrition. This was her first baby and she was overjoyed at bringing him into the world—regardless of the deadbeat father being nowhere in the picture.

Jamaal Baxter was the sorry ass piece of shit she'd been chasing since freshman year in high school. He'd taken Kylie's virginity and was her first real love. He had her wrapped around his finger like a Chinese finger trap, using and abusing her at every turn he possibly could.

Known to be quite the troublemaker, Jamaal was always in and out the joint and he had a bad reputation for owing people money. He'd even done some time in the Feds for fraud. Word was, he'd recently skipped town after failing to pay back a loan shark.

I honestly didn't know why Kylie ever put her trust and heart into the hands of a nigga like him. Everyone knew Jamaal wasn't shit, but Kylie still ended up falling for his weak ass game. Stealing all of the money from her savings account was the last thing he did before going MIA. Now, six months later, here she was, knocked up with his kid. The situation was messed up, and our parents didn't fully approve, but luckily she had their support throughout the pregnancy.

Truth be told, Kylie needed it. She wasn't exactly 'mom material' and she knew it. Kylie was a certified klepto—had been for as long as I could remember. Her desire to steal only increased with age, and oftentimes she found herself on the opposing end of the law. Mama was always having to bail her out the county, and before that it was the juvenile detention center. Secretly, we all hoped and prayed that this baby would eventually change her for the better, because Lord knows she needed it.

From the doorway of the kitchen, I watched as Kylie mingled with close friends and relatives. We'd decided to throw the shower at mama's house since it was big enough to accommodate everyone. She even had a pool out back, though she rarely used it. Mama made good money as a licensed optometrist and daddy owned a truck delivery company. We were blessed to grow up in an upper-middleclass neighborhood out in Alpharetta, Georgia. All of our lives, we'd attended private schools and never wanted for anything. Though our parents weren't together, and hadn't been for years, they were very much equally involved in our lives.

Mama divorced him after finding out that he was having an affair. Surprisingly, she was on her best behavior that day, even though he'd shown up with some white woman that was damn near half his age. It wasn't the woman he'd cheated on mama with, but she was still unwelcomed nevertheless. Fortunately for her, mama decided to spare them both.

When Kylie looked over at me and blew a kiss, a wave of reassurance suddenly washed over me. I'd been the most skeptical about her pregnancy, only because I knew her better than anyone.

Suddenly, the front door opened and in walked my cousin Starr. She was a year older than me and Kylie and had grown up in the same household. As a child, Starr's mother used to pimp her out for drugs until Child Protective Services finally stepped in. Instead of letting her end up in the system, mama volunteered to take care of her.

Trailing close behind Starr was her fine ass boyfriend. Constantine "Cue" Saldana. Like everyone else, they came bearing gifts and congratulatory smiles. As soon as I saw him, I began to feel nervous and anxious. My stomach twisted up in knots and I was as timid as a little girl with a schoolboy crush. I shouldn't have felt that way whenever he was around but I couldn't help it. Cue always had that effect on me, whether he knew it or not.

At 6'2, he was tall and muscular with cinnamon-colored skin. Because of his Afro-Hispanic roots, he had beautiful, soft and fluffy hair that he usually wore pulled back into a lazy ponytail. In addition to his good looks, he had deep set eyes, thick, succulent lips, and a low-pitched voice that made my pussy jump every time he spoke.

I swear he gets sexier every time I see him...

Envy boiled within me since he was with Starr instead of me. Pencil thin with a natural beauty, she was the type of girl every nigga wanted and every chick dreamed of resembling. Honey colored with light brown eyes, piercing dimples, and pouty lips, she looked every bit like a life sized Barbie doll.

Starr was the complete opposite of me. I had been chubby for most of my life, which was how people were easily able to tell me apart from Kylie. Starr, on the other hand, had the kind of likability that attracted men from all walks of life. She was the pretty, fair-skinned girl that guys longed to have on their arm. The kind that you hear about in most rap songs.

How the hell could I compete with that, I asked myself. Suddenly, Cue wrapped his arm around her petite waist, inadvertently reminding me that I never would be able to. He belonged to Starr. They'd been together for three years. Neither one of them were going anywhere anytime soon.

Let that shit go, girl, my conscience whispered.

Kylie immediately cut her eyes at me from across the room and grinned. She was the only person in the world that knew about the crush I had on Cue. Reading her expression, I shook my head, warning her not to start any shit. My sister was famously known for having a big mouth.

Ignoring my gesture, Kylie waddled her fat ass over to me anyway. In the distance, I saw mama giving Starr and Cue hugs. He'd always been close to the family since mama was his father's optometrist.

Cue had left New York at the age of thirteen. Hanging in the streets and constant run-ins with police made his mother fear for his safety and well-being. Due to work, she couldn't supervise him the way he needed so she sent him to live with his father.

We all attended the same high school, which was how he and Starr met. What she didn't know was that I too had been checking for him since the tender age of 12.

"Don't you do it," I told her. The last thing I wanted was to hear her mouth. I knew that me crushing on Cue was strictly prohibited and I didn't need Kylie reminding me. It was already embarrassing enough. I mean, what type of girl regularly fantasized about her cousin's man?

Kylie held her hands up in mock surrender. "*Whaaaat?* I ain't even say nothing," she said innocently. "You the only acting guilty, sis."

"Yeah, 'cuz I know how fond *you* are of acting petty," I laughed.

"Fuck all that. What I wanna know is who invited her to begin with," Kylie said, rolling her eyes. She couldn't stand Starr. It all started after she spread false rumors about Kylie back in high school. It was old news now but my sister just wouldn't let it go.

Ever since she'd moved out, we didn't speak to or deal with her on the regular but we were still cordial for the most part. As adults and as family, we had no other choice. "I didn't either." Starr knew her presence was unnecessary, but that fact alone wasn't enough to keep her from coming. She had a bad habit of showing her face where she wasn't welcomed.

"Well, I certainly ain't send the bitch no invite and she damn sure ain't RSVP—"

"You can stop guessing. You know mama probably sent her the invitation." She was an advocate for keeping the family close, despite any petty rivalries that may've existed among us. For her, family was everything.

"Gossiping ass hoe. That bitch ain't shit and she know she ain't shit," Kylie hissed. "Look at her. Always keeping shit going, talking about other people all the time. Spreading lies like the plague—and about her own damn family at that. I don't see how Cue puts up with her fake ass." Kylie looked like she was ready to pounce on Starr—but her scowl disappeared the moment she and Cue walked up. "Hey, boo!" Kylie said, giving the phoniest smile she could muster up.

Hmph. Now who's fake?

"Damn, cuzzo. You finna pop any day now, I see," Starr said, touching her belly.

"Girl, I'm only six months pergnant," Kylie informed her.

"Get outta here!" she exclaimed. "Sheesh! You're as big as a house!"

"Okay, now apart of me feels like you're calling me fat," Kylie told her. I couldn't tell if she was joking or being serious. Oftentimes, my sister's humor was dry and utterly sarcastic. "You don't know what a woman who's six months looks like?"

Starr giggled. "No, sweetie, I don't. I'm too busy having fun and traveling the world to keep up with the mechanics of child birth." She then threw in some shade for the hell of it. "Besides, I'm not trying to fuck up this perfect figure of mine anytime soon—no offense," she added.

Me and Cue made brief eye contact before I quickly tore my gaze away. Anytime he was around, I felt butterflies in my tummy. He may've belonged to my cousin, but the man had a mystifying control over me.

"What's good, Re-run," he said.

It was a nickname that had been given to me as a child.

"Um...Hey, Cue..." My greeting came out hoarse and I quickly cleared my throat to try again. "How are you?"

"You know a nigga living that life. Ain't no complaints. Shit good wit'chu?"

"Yeah. Few days ago I got an acceptance letter from both Agnes Scott and Spelman College. They were my first and second choice so I'm feeling pretty blessed."

"That's wassup, Khari. Shit that's the move right there. You finna take off. I always knew you'd have a bright future ahead though. You were always one of the most ambitious people I know."

I blushed after his compliment and prayed that Starr didn't notice and call me out on it.

"Thanks," I smiled. "That really means a lot." I felt the same way about him. Clearing my throat again purely out of nervousness, I turned my attention to Starr. "How about you? How've you been?"

"Oh, I'm good, boo. Never been better. Me and Cue just got back from Rio, so a bitch feeling sun-kissed and sexy," she beamed.

Jealousy brewed in the pit of my stomach. I thought I'd detected a tan when she first walked in. For as far back as I could recall, Cue had always done well for himself at only twenty, and he spoiled Starr to no avail. After high school graduation, she became his full-time live in girlfriend and the rest was history.

"That's what's up," I forced out.

"Khari, could you grab the cases of Pepsi out the freezer? There's more guests arriving!"

Mama quickly snapped me out of my thoughts before I ended up hating out loud. "Yeah, ma. No problem," I called back.

Excusing myself from the convo, I headed downstairs to the basement. The distance was just what I needed to remind myself that I was playing with fire. I should not have been thinking about Cue in that way. It just wasn't appropriate—regardless of how fine and engaging he was.

Damn. *Why can't I shake these feelings for this guy?*

Lifting the lid to the freezer, I grabbed the two cases of Pepsi stored inside.

This is starting to get out of hand.

I should've outgrown the crush I had on him but it just never seemed to go away. If anything, it only grew stronger as the years went by. Every time that I was around him, he just did things to me—unexplainable things. He made feel warm and fuzzy inside. He was the only man who'd ever made my heart beat faster and slower.

Eventually you're gonna have to accept that he'll never be yours, I told myself. *No matter how bad you may want him—*

All of a sudden, I heard movement behind me. Startled by the noise, I almost dropped the cases of soda on my feet. When I turned around, Cue was standing there with an impish smirk on his handsome face.

My God, he was sexy.

Immediately, my heart went into overdrive.

"Lemme get that for you," he offered.

When Cue grabbed the cases of soda from me, his fingers lightly brushed against mine. An electric jolt shot throughout my body before settling right in between my thighs. *Lord, give me strength*, I prayed.

He was close enough to smell the Armani cologne. Close enough to kiss even...

After getting a handle on the cases, he turned around and started for the staircase. I didn't release the breath I was holding until he was finally out of view.

Smiling to myself, I shook my head in total disbelief. In that brief moment, I was actually foolish enough to think that he might just kiss me. That our attraction might have been mutual...Wishful thinking I suppose.

Maybe in another lifetime.

1

KHARI

PRESENT DAY

With my 7-year old son Ali in tow, I carefully made my way to the visits hall where my fiancé awaited our arrival. This was only Ali's third time visiting his father in prison, because I hated him having to see his dad locked up. Normally, I didn't bring him with me to visitation but Aubrey insisted. He claimed his family was the only thing keeping him sane behind prison walls, so I refused to rob him of the privilege of being a father to his only child.

When me and Ali entered the somewhat noisy hall, we found Aubrey sitting alone at an empty stainless steel table, surrounded by fellow inmates and their chatty relatives. My smile widened as I approached him and he graciously returned it. He had a fresh cut and his face was groomed. It was nice to see that he was taking care of himself. I couldn't front. Even for a convicted felon, Aubrey looked good.

At 35, he was ten years older than me, dark chocolate, and somewhat rough around the edges. He had big, brown eyes, long lashes, and thick, juicy lips. There was a small scar along his jaw and one that ran through his left eyebrow that he told me was from a bar fight years ago.

Flaws aside, Aubrey was devilishly

handsome. Slim, tall, and toned in build, he reminded me of an NBA player in his prime. Aubrey had always been a gym rat and he made sure it showed in his physique.

Covering over 60% of his body was a collage of decorative tattoos. The only areas that weren't tatted was his face and neck. His favorite one of all was the portrait of Ali on his upper arm. Our son was his proudest accomplishment.

Aubrey quickly stood to his feet to greet us. "*Waa gwaan, empress*," he said in a thick Caribbean accent. He was born and raised in St. Thomas and relocated to the U.S. ten years ago. "It's been a minute since I seen ya'll." Pulling me and Ali towards him, Aubrey hugged us tightly. It'd been almost four months to be exact, and although I wanted to see him more, work and school simply wouldn't permit it. Taking time off for the 3 ½ hour drive from Atlanta to Savannah was easier said than done.

"I tried to get out here last week but my schedule was hectic—"

"Guess what? You here though. That's all that matters. Not to mention, I had to prepare myself mentally before we linked up."

I could respect that he wanted to have his mind right before he dealt with me. We all took our respectful seats, with Ali sitting closest to Aubrey. He was unashamedly a daddy's boy since Aubrey spoiled him. Ali gave a snaggle-tooth grin after his father playfully ruffled his short, curly hair. He had my hazel eyes, coffee complexion, and dimpled chin. Everyone said that he was a spitting image of me.

"So...how are you holding up?" I asked. It was nearly two years since Aubrey was arrested on drug and weapon charges. This was his third strike, so the judge and jury didn't cut him any slack at trial. I almost fainted in court when they read his sentencing. Ever since he'd left, my life just hadn't been the same.

"Same shit, different day."

Ali excitedly communicated through hand gestures. He was born with congenital hearing loss due to pregnancy complications. Aubrey never wanted Ali to feel different from other children so he overindulged when it came to spoiling him. Our son had all of the latest high tech gadgets, game consoles, and every special edition shoe known to man. Aubrey cherished his son and spared no expense when it came to him. He was a damn good father, which was why I'd stayed with him for as long as I did, in spite of his constant infidelities.

Prior to his imprisonment, Aubrey had a real problem with keeping his dick in his pants. As a well-known music producer and party host, he was always surrounded by aspiring models, artists, and thirsty hoes looking for a quick come up. There were some side chicks out there willing to do anything for the limelight. It wasn't until I threatened to leave him for good that Aubrey finally straightened up his act and proposed to me.

"Ali just said he misses you a lot." Since Aubrey was always in the streets or at the studio, he never bothered to learn sign language. Luckily for him, Ali was an expert when it came to reading lips. "Sometimes he wakes up thinking that you're still there," I told him. "Sometimes I do too…"

"You know you gotta nigga deep in his feelings about ya'll," Aubrey said. Pulling his son close, he kissed the top of his head.

It was a few weeks until Christmas and I hated that he wouldn't be home for the holidays. I could tell he was saddened that he couldn't physically be there for us.

"Have you heard anything from the lawyer?" I asked, changing the subject. We'd been working on an appeal ever since his conviction.

Aubrey scoffed and rolled his eyes. He hated whenever I brought up legal matters during visitation. "Nah…but don't trouble yaself about it, y' hear? A real nigga gon' stand where a real nigga land. As long as my family's good I ain't gon' ever lose sleep."

"Aubrey, by the time you get out your son will practically be an adult," I reminded him. "How could you sleep peacefully knowing that you'll miss out on him growing up?"

"You said the key thing…when I get out. You know they can't keep a real nigga down for long. I'mma still be there for him no matter what."

"How can you be there for him when you're in here?!" I yelled.

With a concerned expression, Ali asked if I were okay. He wasn't accustomed to seeing me lose my cool, and I prided myself on my patience. Simmering down a bit before I caused a scene, I raked a hand through my naturally curly hair and sighed. I hated for my son to see me worked up but our current state of affairs was ultimately taking its toll on me. Aubrey had been gone for over a year and I still wasn't used to his absence. Forcing a smile, I told Ali that I was fine in sign language.

He had no idea that it was a lie.

In fact, I was gradually falling apart. I never anticipated on raising our child alone. Because I had grown up in a two parent household, I wanted the same for our son. And as thankful as I was for the lifestyle Aubrey gave us, I would've chosen him over it any day.

Sensing my frustrations, he reached over and placed his hand over mine. The simple gesture alone made me relax a little. Aubrey had a knack for making me feel secure.

I met Aubrey while waitressing part-time at a family owned diner. I'd just started my freshman year in college and needed the extra money for books. He and his brother visited one day during lunch hours. They'd only been living in the states for three months at the time of our introduction.

Truthfully, I didn't immediately find Aubrey attractive. He was scruffy looking, overly confident, and a tad bit aggressive. But over time, I grew to love everything about him. He helped mold me into the woman I was today. He taught me a lot, and he was the first and only man I'd ever truly loved. With that being said, I eventually got over the crush I had on Cue. He moved to New York just before I went off to school and I never saw him again.

"I'm locked up, but my money ain't. You think these bars gon' stop a nigga from getting money? These bars ain't stopping shit. If anything, these bars taught me how to network better," he explained. "Can't shit stop me from taking care of my family."

There was a long period of silence between us before he spoke again.

"You still be in the church every Sunday?" Aubrey asked.

I'd been attending the Sunday services at our local church devotedly. I even helped organize some of the special events. "Yes," I answered. "Every week."

"Aight, then have faith that shit's gon' get greater later."

Something about his words gave me hope. And he was right. He really did do everything he could to take care of his family. He may've been imprisoned, but his revenue consistently poured in like he was still in the streets.

Aubrey ran a lucrative drug business outside of his music career. He even he had a few loyal customers that were in the industry. Every month, he received packages that were shipped to different people's houses, and the niggas on his payroll sold the work on the streets.

Aubrey never had that shit around us; he never even had a shipment delivered to our house. He didn't want us exposed to his lifestyle, and I was fine with that because I'd never condoned him selling drugs in the first place. Since it was our main source of income I couldn't quite complain either. After all, it was the same money that funded my education.

Mama would've been so disappointed if she ever found out the truth about Aubrey. I had told her that he was arrested for failing to pay taxes. She didn't know about his life as a dealer. For years she'd been under the impression that he was nothing more than a music producer. Mama would've shunned me if she knew I'd fallen in love with a criminal.

As much as I wanted to confide in her, I knew that I couldn't. Mama already wasn't too fond Aubrey because of the issues I'd spoken to her about in the past. I mean, how could she respect a man who constantly lied, cheated, and abused her daughter?

Mama told me time and time again to leave him alone but I just couldn't. Honestly, this street shit and Aubrey's thugged out mentality turned me on. He made me feel important, like I was that bitch. Not to mention, he laid it down like a beast in the bedroom. He had me so gone that I didn't want to return. He had me sprung like a box mattress. Everything about him captivated me.

Aubrey was street, but he was also wise, patient, and clever. Being with him was like a breath of fresh air. Because he was older, he was a lot more mature than the young fuck boys I used to entertain. He'd gotten me at a young age and groomed me into the woman and mother I was today.

Shaking off those worrisome feelings, I caressed his hand and smiled. "I'll try to have faith..." It was the best I could come up with.

Aubrey sensed my uncertainty. "You can't try to have faith. You gotta *believe*," he stressed.

After several minutes of small talk and reminiscing, a C.O. finally notified everyone that visiting hours were over. Ali sulked and pouted since we had to leave, but I reminded him that we'd be back next month.

When Aubrey pulled me in for a firm, farewell hug, he whispered in my ear, "Make sure you keep things in line. We don't need you falling off track."

I knew exactly what he meant by that.

"Aubrey, I'm too busy working and raising your son to be out here entertaining other men."

"That's real, stay focused," he said. "Do you think you can do me a favor though? You think you can cover my shit up next time you come here...'fore I have to *kill* one of these niggas." Out of nowhere, Aubrey snapped on one of his fellow inmates. "*Wah di bumboclaat wrang wid yu*!?" I assumed the man was from the islands as well since he'd started speaking broken English. The older man had been checking me out ever since I walked in.

"How 'bout I just wear a black trash bag instead," I said sarcastically.

Aubrey squeezed my ass and pulled me towards him. "Alright now," he said as if he were warning me. "*Mmm*." He gave my butt another firm squeeze and Ali quickly covered his eyes. He never cared to see our affection. "Dat mufucka back there gettin' fat," he teased. "I'mma have to make a way to get up in that. So the next time you come make sure you don't have no panties on."

With a flirtatious grin, I told him, "How about we just focus on one thing at a time."

Thankfully, my chubbiness transitioned into a curvy and voluptuous shape. I rocked a size sixteen with pride, but the extra weight was in all the right places. Everyone said that I had Ali to thank for that.

"Alright, queen." Aubrey kissed my

forehead. Tilting my chin up to meet his gaze, he stared lovingly into my eyes. "I don't wanna have to wait long to see that pretty smile again."

"I promise you won't."

Aubrey ruffled his son's hair again before giving him a final hug. After saying our goodbyes, we parted ways.

"Bless up yaself," Aubrey called after me.

Right about now, I needed all of the blessings I could get if I planned on holding him down for this ten-year stretch. Looking down at my son, I suddenly had doubts about marrying a man in prison.

Would things get better? Would things get worse?

I had no idea how to cope with this shit and I wasn't sure where my life was going. Not to mention, I had a child to think about. It wasn't fair for me to drag him through this shit. Men could make things sound really good at rehearsal, but the outcome could be entirely different.

All of a sudden, I began to have doubts about everything in general. It was the first time since Aubrey's conviction that I actually questioned myself as well as my moralities.

2
KYLIE

I got broads in Atlanta…

Twisting dope, lean, and the Fanta…

Credit cards and scammers…

Hitting off licks in the bando…

Black X6, Phantom…

White X6 looks like a panda…

Going out like I'm Montana…

Hundred killers, hundred hammers…

My best friend Paige multi-tasked between twerking and smoking a blunt to Desiigner's *Panda*. She was a cute, slender Puerto-Rican girl, originally from the Flatbush area of Brooklyn, New York.

Paige was my partner in crime. We'd met in jail a couple years back and were both there for petty theft. Everyone—including my sister—thought she was a bad influence but I didn't give a fuck. I was a grown ass woman, free to make my own choice in friends.

Just then, Paige took off her leggings to watch her booty jiggle and shake in the full length mirror. Her pink Hello Kitty draws were riding insanely high up her ass while she danced but she obviously thought that shit was cute. Paige was a ho, who'd seen more cocks than the walls of a sperm bank.

Thankfully, my bedroom door was closed. I knew how much the trap music and smell of weed bothered mama. Also, she wasn't particularly fond of Paige. She and Khari loved pretending they were holier than thou. They never liked my men, friends, or lifestyle. Oh well, fuck 'em.

At 25, I was still living at home. After losing the baby at 7 months, I just gave up on most shit in life, including independence. Khari went on to get a degree and have a kid while I pretty much stayed stagnant. The miscarriage had fucked me all the way up. I'd even started popping Percocet and stealing again just to fill the void inside of me. No one was happier than me about the pregnancy...and when my son died, I just lost it. I lost myself.

"What do you think about me getting ass shots?" Paige asked, interrupting my thoughts.

"Hoe, I'm thinking about that yeast infection you finna be stuck with. Anyway, we need to be focused on *making* money instead of spending it," I reminded her. "Speaking of which, how much you think we can get for all this shit?"

Laid across my mattress was all of the designer purses, expensive perfumes, and clothes we'd stolen from Nordstrom's a few hours earlier. Boosting had become my way of life.

Paige took a final puff on the blunt before passing it to me. "Hmm..." She looked over every item carefully while doing the math in her head. "Roughly, I'd say...close to a grand."

I sighed exasperatedly. "*Ugh*! That's it?! Bitch, I need a lick! Not this chump change we been making. I'm tired of Uber and riding the fucking bus. I need a car, bitch." The days of borrowing money from mama were over since I'd burned my bridges there. I had to make sure I was able to support me by any means necessary.

Paige placed a finger on her chin like she was thinking. "If we try to upsell—"

"*Upsell*?! Bitch, ain't nobody 'bout to spend big money on some yoga pants and Michael Kors bags. See, I told ya ass we should've hit one of them luxury stores like Gucci or Celine. But noooo, you ain't want to—"

"Dummy, that shit be secured as fuck. Plus, they got cameras like a mothafucka—"

"Lock-picking is my forte...and fuck a camera. I'll wear a hoodie or something," I argued. "Them bitches be running a couple grand easy. We could rack up a few thousands apiece with no sweat if we snagged a few."

"I don't know," Paige said, doubtfully. "Shit, I'm all for making a come up, but ain't nobody trying to go to jail. Hell, I just *got off* probation."

"Hoe, ain't *nobody* going to jail."

"Well, I say you go for it and let me know how that works out."

I rolled my eyes at Paige and shook my head. Sometimes she could be such a pussy. "You real crusty for that shit."

She opened her mouth to say something but was interrupted by the doorbell ringing. I almost expected mama to answer until I remembered that she and her boyfriend, Lenny were on a three-day cruise in the Bahamas. "All I'm asking is for you to think about it. Okay?" I said on my way out the room.

Padding barefoot to the front door, I stood on my tiptoes and looked through the peephole. Much to my surprise, there was no one standing on the other end. "What the hell?"

Chalking it up to some bad ass kids in the 'hood, I turned and walked away—

Ding dong.

Growling in frustration, I stomped back to the front of the house. When I looked through the peephole again there was still no one there. Fed up with the bullshit, I swung the door open in anger. "Look, whoever the fuck is playing on my gotdamn—"

All of a sudden, someone reached out and grabbed me.

3

KYLIE

A calloused hand clamped tightly over my mouth before I could scream for help. As I struggled in my captor's embrace, I felt his erection pressing into the small of my back. *Oh my God, this nigga about to rape me!* My throat stung as I desperately tried to call Paige's name. It was useless since my mouth was covered.

When I recognized who was holding me I finally calmed down. "Jamaal! You fucking asshole!" Never in a million years did I expect to see my ex. Then again, he had a habit of coming out the cut like Cosby victims.

Whap!

I hit him as hard as I could in the chest as he laughed hysterically like seeing me scared was the funniest shit on earth.

"It's not funny, Jamaal! You childish as fuck!"

Whap!

I hit him again, this time across his face. In one fluid motion, he grabbed my wrist and snatched me so close to him that our bodies were pressed together.

"That rough shit only makes my dick hard."

Disgusted by his words and mere

presence, I pushed him away. "Boy, I wouldn't fuck you or any nigga that resembles you. And why the hell do you play so much? You almost gave me a damn heart attack! What is wrong with you? I seriously could've hurt you—"

"Man, hold that noise and gimme that tongue to suck on."

Jamaal leaned in to kiss me but I quickly moved away. *"Hell naw*! I don't know where the fuck your tongue been. Besides, it ain't even that type of party no more, Mall. It's been years since I last saw you. You always in and out. You can't just pop the fuck up whenever you feel like it and expect to get some mothafucking ass."

"Aww, girl, cut the games. You know you miss it."

"Nah, nigga. Run me that mothafucking money you owe me. That's what I'm missing."

Jamaal chuckled, clearly amused by my feistiness. He always told me my mouth was too smart for a soft nigga. "You real funny, you know that shit." He smiled, revealing his deep set of dimples. I always told him he reminded me of Juelz Santana but with dreads. Jamaal wasn't shit half the time, but the man was unquestionably fine. He was also trouble.

Eyeing the fresh fit and jewelry he had on, I quickly realized that he wasn't the same broke nigga I fell in love with. Everything was designer from the Versace shades perched on top of his head to the matching sneakers on his feet.

"You standing here looking like new money and shit, where my mothafucking cut at?" I asked.

"Man, calm down with all that shit, girl. Why you think I'm here?" Jamaal pulled off his Louis Vuitton backpack and handed it to me. "Real niggas do real shit."

After unzipping the bag, I eagerly peeked inside. Gasping in shock, I covered my mouth and looked up at Jamaal. There was a shitload of money in the backpack, each stack bundled tightly and labeled $10,000. If I had to guess, I'd say there was at least half a million present and accounted for.

"Damn, Jamaal. Where the hell did you get this kind of cash?"

"The details ain't important."

"Jamaal, I—are you for real? Boy, do not fucking play with me!" He only owed me $2,000 but I would've gladly taken all the money if he really was giving it to me. "I can have all of this? Are you serious? Are you fucking serious?"

"Dead ass."

"Jamaal...Oh my God! This is fucking incredible! Thank you! Thank you! Thank you God knows I really need this money! Oh my God!" Snatching out a single stack, I made it rain on my gotdamn self.

"Wait a minute, bitch...I'mma need you to calm the fuck down. Now there *is* one catch."

I sucked my teeth and blew out air. "Oh, boy, here we go." My mama said if something seemed too good to be true it probably was. "There's always a fucking catch when it comes to you. Well then...what is it?"

"Looks can be deceiving."

"What do you mean by that?"

"It looks real...but it's counterfeit."

"WHAT! Are you fucking serious? Boy, get the fuck outta here. What type of fool do you take me for?" Tossing the bag at his feet, I prepared to slam the door right in his damn face.

"Hol' up, hol' up...before you get so judgmental about it, I'mma need you to hear me out first." Jamaal quickly grabbed my elbow and turned me around.

"What else is there to say, Jamaal? You brought this fake ass money here thinking you was gon' get back in my good graces. I don't know who's stupider. You or me for believing you were really finna give me half a mil."

"But I guarantee every bill in that mufucka passes for the real thing," he said. "Go head. Pull out a band, thumb through it. You won't find a single defect. I put that on blood."

"And I'm supposed to believe that?"

"Look at it. Shit, that's all you gotta do."

Sighing deeply, I reached down, grabbed a stack of money from the bag, and looked closely at it. As sure as shit, it had the official blue band across every hundred. There wasn't a single imperfection in sight. The bills were absolutely flawless.

"You sure it'll pass for real?" I asked.

"Take that shit to the bank. You'll see."

"How could you be so sure? Have you tried to spend any of this money?"

"Go outside and look in the driveway."

Parked in front of the house was a brand new pearl white BMW convertible. It had a peanut butter wood grain interior, a fresh wax job, and custom Forgiatos rims that were at least six grand a piece. On the top of the hood was a huge, red bow.

"Fresh off the lot," he bragged. "The best for the best."

I hadn't even noticed the car until he pointed it out. "Oh, my God, Jamaal! You gotta be fucking kidding me! OH MY GOD! You bought me a car?!" I shouted with enthusiasm. "Hell yeah!" I was in complete shock and disbelief. I couldn't wait to floss and show out in my new car.

"Think of it as a peace offering." Jamaal pulled my face towards him. "Look, I know you think a nigga be on some bullshit. But now I got some shit that's gon' make everything right."

I wanted to believe he was being sincere, but the nigga had good ass penitentiary game. Jamaal was a habitual liar and a womanizer, who constantly sold dreams. "Jamaal...you know it's hard for me to trust you. You talking all this big shit now but you good for going MIA. Don't build me up just to tear me down—"

"Nah, we all the way to the top from here on out. No ceilings, baby. Enough of the games, a nigga tryin' to be on some real shit wit'chu."

"Yeah, I bet you are now that it's convenient for you. How do I know you ain't gon' be on that bullshit again?"

"Gimme a chance to prove it to you."

Because I felt myself getting emotional I quickly changed the topic. I hated for anyone—especially a man—to see me vulnerable. "Is this shit like...for real official? I mean like...*for real* for real? I won't run into any trouble spending this money, right? There won't be any problems?" I was still on probation so I had to tread very carefully.

"That money gon' spend itself."

"So I'm good?"

"You're great," Jamaal assured me. "Now can I get some of that mufuckin' tongue?"

"Nigga please. You ain't out the mothafucking doghouse yet."

"You still petty as fuck I see."

"Nah, I'm *real* as fuck."

4

STARR

Laying acrylic on my client Lisa's nails, I listened as she vented about her cheating ass no good man. Every time she sat in my chair it was the same old sad song. Since I loved drama and gossip, the shit was pure entertainment to me—especially since I was fucking him too. Her nigga was a big time local rapper who slept with any bitch that looked in his direction. He had money but he made it clear that wifey was going nowhere so I played the game for what it was worth.

Lisa wasn't the only client whose man I'd slept with. I had fucked at least half of their husbands at one time or another in life. My reputation preceded me.

After Cue dumped my ass several years ago, I just let loose. I started partying, drinking heavy, and fucking with street niggas. I lost my self-respect and discipline when he left.

Let Cue tell it I would only hold him back from accomplishing his goals. Our heads were in two different places at the time. I wanted things to stay the same while he craved change and the freedom to spread his wings. In order to make that happen, he moved back to New York City. Last I heard, he had a new bitch and was living lavish in Manhattan.

Damn. Cue....

I couldn't even flex. I still thought about his fine ass from time to time. He was one of the best things that ever happened to me and no one had ever treated me quite like him. Hands down, he was the best nigga that I ever came in contact with.

Right now, I dealt with someone new but he wasn't on Cue's level. We were just kicking it, having fun and seeing where shit went. I wasn't ready to get serious with anybody because as much as I hated to admit it, I hadn't fully gotten over my first heartbreak.

Lost in thoughts about what might have been, I didn't notice the suspicious intruder entering the shop. The bell above the door chimed, and I assumed it was another walk-in. Boy was I wrong.

The sudden sound of a loaded gun being cocked grabbed everyone's attentions. When I looked up from my desk, I saw a man dressed in all black wearing a ski mask with the mouth cut out. In his hands was a sawed off shotgun. My heart plummeted to the pit of my stomach. We were being robbed.

Before I could grab my phone to call the police, he ran over and pressed his gun to my head. I figured he'd chosen me since my desk was closest to the door. "I need everybody to throw they purses, cellphones, and jewelry in the middle of floor. Anybody that tries anything I'll blow this bitch's mufuckin' head off!"

Since customers were slow to realize what was happening, he let me go and grabbed a nearby child. A girl who was no older than ten or eleven.

"Ya'll think this a mothafucking game?!"

BAM!

He clocked her in the head with the butt of his shotgun.

"I said throw the mufuckin' shit in the middle of the floor 'fore I blow this lil' bitch's brains out!"

Blood gushed from a gash on the little girl's forehead. She was crying and screaming at the top of her lungs.

"Oh my God, that's my baby!" the girl's mother cried out. She quickly ran over towards them to protect her child.

POW!

A shotgun blast to the chest stopped her dead in her tracks. The impact and amount of pellets opened her up wide. Blood, tissue, and bits of organs splattered onto nearby customers—including her own daughter who passed out from shock.

Everyone scrambled to pull off their jewelry and hand it over now that they knew he wasn't fucking around. Frozen in fear by what I'd witnessed, I sat there in complete disbelief.

"Hurry the fuck up before another one of

ya'll bitches get opened up!"

Toting a small, black trash bag, the self-entitled son of a bitch collected everyone's valuables. When he saw that I failed to give in to his demands, he pointed his gun at me. "Bitch, you hard of fucking hearing?"

Since I wasn't trying to be his next victim, I quickly snatched off my necklace and diamond tennis bracelet. I was just about to pull my ring off too until I remembered that it held sentimental value. The ring once belonged to my great-grandmother, who passed it down to her daughter, who passed it down to hers. Eventually, it found its way into my possession. It meant a lot to me, and I would've died before handing it over.

"Bitch, I said take it all off! That means that mufuckin' rock on ya finger too!" he yelled, waving his gun in my face.

"I—I can't give it to you! It belonged to my grandmother! Please, it's the only thing I have left of hers—"

"Do I gotta make an example outta you?"

Tears poured down my cheeks as I cried like a baby. I was so terrified that I was shaking uncontrollably. This would definitely go down in history as one of the worst days of my life. What type of nigga went around robbing nail salons? This shit just wasn't happening.

"Please! I'm begging you—"

WHAP!

My sentence was interrupted when his fist connected with my face. He hit me so hard that everything immediately went fuzzy and then completely black.

5
STARR

After I was treated by medical personnel, I gave a written statement to police and headed home without my grandmother's ring. It was safe to say that I wouldn't be going in to work tomorrow with everything that'd happened today.

The thirty-minute drive back home was long and thwarted by rush hour traffic. When I finally reached my exit I breathed a deep sigh of relief. I couldn't wait to pour a shot of Avion and fire up a blunt. As I bent the corner to the block I lived on, I noticed a black Acura sitting in the driveway of my home.

A smile tugged at my lips since I recognized the vehicle almost immediately. Parking directly behind him, I turned off the engine and climbed out. As I approached his car, I knew right away he was blowing on some gas— and without me at that.

Opening the passenger door, I climbed in and greeted him with a passionate kiss. There was still dried blood on my face from the woman he'd shot but he didn't seem to mind at all. It was a small price to pay in order to make the set up seem legit.

Shane still had his ski mask on. The trash bag of jewelry and money sat in the backseat.

Every time we hit a lick together, he came straight to the crib so that we could divide everything 50/50.

Before the salons, we used to set up drug dealers and any niggas we knew had money. By the time we exhausted that outlet, we had no choice but to switch up things so we started robbing businesses. The licks were sweet. We'd been making such a come up that we had no intentions of retiring anytime soon.

They way we orchestrated the set ups were simple. After personally profiling each location, I'd get a job at a popular, big name salon where dope boys' girlfriends and wives of rappers were known to frequent. Shane and I only hit places that were bringing in a lot of high-paying clientele. We always knew we'd hit the jackpot with every lick. We had a system to ensure that every robbery was successful and worth it.

Once every lick was complete, I quit the job citing emotional distress from the robbery. It was the perfect excuse for a clean getaway.

"Wassup, baby?"

"Starr, you know I ain't mean to knock you out but I had to make shit look authentic," he smiled. Shane's voice reminded of the Game's. It was deep and raspy in pitch. "I would never wanna do anything to fuck up that pretty face of yours." Shane tilted my head to the side to see the damage. My cheek was still a bit puffy and red. Because I was mixed, I had light skin that bruised easily.

Taking his hand, I slid his finger inside my mouth. "I keep telling you I'mma big girl..." With my free hand, I rubbed his erection through his jeans. "You know every time you put your hands on me it turns me on."

Shane licked his lips. He loved when I talked nasty. "Bitch, you gon' make me fuck you right here." That crazy shit turned him on too.

Reaching for his Hermes belt, I unbuckled his jeans. Seeing him take charge the way he did earlier made my pussy soaking wet. "Seeing you kill that bitch like that had me ready to fuck you right there, in the middle of all the commotion."

"Well, shit, ain't no time like the present, baby."

That was all I needed to hear in order to hike up my maxi dress and straddle him. Shane groaned softly as my juicy pussy slid over his thick, rock hard dick.

"Damn, bitch..."

"How's it feel?" I asked, bouncing up and down in his lap.

"Tight, deep, and wet as fuck. You know you got that A-1." Shane wrapped a hand around my throat and kissed me. "This my pussy?"

"Yes," I moaned.

"This my pussy?" he asked again to be certain. "Bitch, don't fuck with me."

"Yes, baby. It's all yours."

We shouldn't have been fucking reckless and raw but the sex was too good to think rationally. The possibility of getting pregnant or catching something didn't come to mind either—even though Shane was a well known hoe in the streets. The nigga was for everybody and yet I couldn't leave his ass alone. Not when we were making so much money together.

Reclining the seat, I got a bit more comfortable so I could ride him just the way he liked it. "Damn, bitch. You finna make this mufucka spit early. Slow the fuck down."

"Nah, keep up," I said, riding faster.

Shane squeezed on my ass. "Shit, Starr...pussy so good you make a nigga wanna pay for this shit."

All of a sudden, I felt my climax building up. "*Mmm*, damn..." Biting my lip, I whispered, "I'm finna cum."

"Gon' 'head. Ride that dick, baby. Ride that dick 'til you bust. I'mma cum right wit'chu."

"*Nuhhh*...you can't come inside me this time."

Shane's grip around my throat tightened. "I own you! Don't tell me what the fuck I can't do with my pussy," he growled. "You *my* mufuckin' bitch. This *my* mufuckin' pussy."

Suddenly, a wave of euphoria rushed over

me just as Shane released his load deep inside. My moans were loud enough to wake the dead when I came. No one could fuck me like Shane—other than Cue of course.

Winded and fatigued, I collapsed against his muscular chest panting heavily. For several seconds, we simply held one another and kissed passionately.

"I told you not to cum in me," I whined. "You hardheaded as fuck. You know I ain't trying to get pregnant."

"What's so fucked up about having a kid with me?" he asked curiously.

"You see this body?" I seductively ran my hands down my shapely figure. "Ain't no babies coming out this bitch." It was my prized possession. My meal ticket—as my mother would say. "Besides, you already got six mothafucking kids. You need to start wrapping that fertile meat of yours. I swear you got the worst pull out game ever."

Shane broke out laughing.

"I ain't about to be your third damn baby mama."

"Shit, you know what they say. Three's a charm."

I waved him off. "Fuck outta here, nigga. You better run that shit by another bitch 'cuz I ain't trying to hear it."

I blamed my finances for the reason why I didn't want children. But the truth was motherhood absolutely terrified me. My own had treated me so shitty that I never knew what a real mom was like.

I quickly shook the thoughts from my mind before I got caught up in old, painful memories. The shit was in the past and belonged right there.

Reaching in the backseat of the car, I grabbed the trash bag and fished around for my ring. What I'd told Shane earlier in the salon wasn't just for show. It really was the only thing I owned that belonged to that poor ass excuse of a mother. When I finally found it, I pulled it out and slipped it back on my finger.

6
KHARI

Ali and I had just returned from grocery shopping when I noticed an unfamiliar car parked in front of my home. I found it odd because there weren't many people who knew where we lived. Aubrey was very private about his personal life and he'd taught me to be the same way.

"Who the hell is this?" I asked myself aloud.

I prayed that the Feds weren't still sniffing around. While fighting his case, Aubrey never mentioned anyone in connection to him. Authorities knew he was getting his product from someone, they just didn't know from who. Prior to his trial, they offered him a deal if he gave up names to help them take down everyone he was working with. Aubrey wasn't a snitch though, and he took his L like a champ—alone.

I could remember being so upset with him for not cooperating, especially since we were promised witness protection. Regardless of how tempting their offer was, Aubrey didn't budge, no matter how many times I had to remind him about his family.

Just give them the names, I'd say over the phone every time he called from jail. Aubrey was a firm believer of the no snitching policy, so he ended up taking the fall for everyone in connection. He refused to turn in the others just to save his own ass. He just wasn't that type of guy.

After pulling into my driveway, I turned off the engine. Looking at the side view mirror, I watched as a woman climbed out the driver's seat. She didn't look like a cop or anyone in that field but I could've been wrong.

Me and Ali climbed out together, with him slamming the door a bit too hard for comfort. His father had a bad habit of doing it as well.

"Hello. Can I help you?" I asked the woman. She appeared to be in her early to mid-twenties. She had dark brown skin, a short pixie cut, and curvy figure. She reminded me of the singer, Fantasia.

There was a perturbed look on my face as I waited on her answer. I'd never seen her before so I couldn't say I knew the reason behind her visit, though something told me it wasn't pleasant.

"I think it's time we talked woman to woman." She looked from me to Ali as she spoke.

I noticed that there was a small boy in her backseat. He and Ali looked close in age. "Ali, go in the house," I told him.

"...Okay." He seemed uncertain about the strange and suspicious woman before me Still, he obediently did as he was told.

After making sure that he was safe inside,

I turned back towards the uninvited guest. She looked emotional and distraught about something. "Do you mind me asking who his father is?"

"Do you mind me asking you what concern that is of yours?" I rebutted.

"Nah boo. I don't think you know who I am."

"Should I?"

Folding her arms, she gave me a look of pure disgust. "For years, I knew about the other bitches...but I had no idea that a child was involved."

"No honey, you don't know who *I* am. And again, I ask you, what does my child have to do with this?" She was starting to sound like a crazy, old bat.

"I need to know," she pressed. "I just need the truth. What is his father's name?" There was desperation in her eyes as she begged me for answers.

Her presence alone gave me an uncomfortable feeling. I just knew this young bitch was trouble. "Who are you and why the hell are you on my property? You got sixty seconds to answer or I'm calling the police."

I should've realized this had something to do with Aubrey. This damn sure wouldn't be the first time some random bitch popped up on my doorstep looking to fight over a man that couldn't even be faithful. Little did I know, she wasn't just some random bitch.

"I'm the mother of Aubrey's child," she stated.

The bomb she dropped on me left me in complete shambles. For a minute, I thought I'd misheard her. Did she *really* just say what I think she did? "What the hell are you talking about? Aubrey only has one child and it's with me."

"I beg to differ," she said, proudly pulling out a birth certificate. She handed it over in a read 'em and weep sort of fashion and I angrily snatched the paper out her hand. Sure enough, Aubrey's signature was there, clear as day for any non-believers to see. Her son was born two years after Ali—while me and Aubrey were still very much together.

I almost wanted to faint. My knees buckled beneath me. I felt a hard lump in my throat that I couldn't swallow for the life of me. Accepting the truth hurt like hell. The thought of Ali having another sibling left me null and void. How could Aubrey do this to me and sit back and act like everything was normal?

I can't believe this mothafucka been knowing this for years and hasn't said shit about it.

Aubrey's baby mama, Leah held her hand out for the paper. Now that I had proof she wanted her shit back.

I wanted to rip the birth certificate in half and then set it on fire. I was that pissed off! The nerve of this bitch to show up and hit me with something like this.

My gaze shifted to her son. If it wasn't for him being there I might've acted irate. Swallowing my dignity, I handed Leah back the certificate as tears welled up in my eyes. I quickly blinked them away. I wouldn't dare let this bitch see me shed a tear over Aubrey's sorry ass.

"You ready to talk like women now?" she asked.

7
KHARI

I agreed to talk to Leah since I had a few questions of my own so I decided to meet with her at *Piedmont Park*. If we were going to talk, we had to do it on neutral grounds. I didn't feel comfortable with her coming to my home, discussing my man.

Despite the circumstances, it was a bright, sunny day for a quick stroll. People were out with their picnic blankets, pets, and children—and there we were, in the middle of it all, because of a common denominator we shared.

Aubrey.

"First off, I think we've been sharing the same man for years," Leah said. "I'm quite sure that whenever he wasn't with me he was with you and when he wasn't with you he was with me. Lately, I've been noticing his patterns changing. He's always rearranging his visitation days. He hasn't been asking me for the things he normally does and I assume its because he's getting it from you. He also hasn't been calling as much as he usually does. And then when I came to visit him last week, I saw your name on the sign-in sheet. That's how I found out about you," she explained. "I hate to admit it, but I've been watching you for a while now. The other day I saw you drop off your son at school— He never even told me he had another child—"

"Trust and believe, it's a lot of things you don't know."

"Well, how about we enlighten each other."

***

My nights were restless after learning that Aubrey had another woman he'd been seeing long term. Every time I closed my eyes I envisioned him being with her the exact same way he's been with me. And to make matters worse, he had another kid. That fact alone kept me up into the wee hours of the morning.

I hardly got any work done over the next few days. The bomb she dropped on me just kept playing over and over in my head. I had to figure out how I was going to approach the situation.

I'd given Aubrey over eight years of my life. I even bore him a son. How could he ever keep something like that hidden from me? It had my stomach in knots.

I didn't want to believe that he had been playing me for so long. But then again, we were engaged for five years with no definite date for the wedding. It made me wonder if he was planning to marry her as well. Suddenly, I felt like an idiot. But I guess everybody plays the fool.

I had to hear the truth from the horse's mouth, so I planned a visit to see Aubrey that weekend. That time, I decided to travel solo, leaving Ali with his 18-year old babysitter Sharon. The drive to the Federal prison was three hours, and by the time I got there I still didn't know what I was going to say to him.

After sign-in and going through the routine search, I was finally taken to the visits hall where I found him sitting near the window. Aubrey looked elated to see me, but there was no smile present on my face considering the circumstances. We had to talk. I needed the truth more than anything.

"*Whap'am*, queen," he greeted. Aubrey stood to hug me and I couldn't even bring myself to return the affection. It took everything in me not to put my hands on him.

"There's some explaining you need to do," I said, getting straight to the point.

Aubrey's smile slowly vanished. Noticing the irritation in my tone, he sensed that something was amidst. After pulling out my chair for me he took his seat. "About?"

"First, is there anything you have to tell me before I open my mouth?"

"Is there anything you'd *like* me to tell you?"

"Malik. Does that name ring a bell?" I asked him.

Aubrey became stone-faced. His expression said it all.

"Is there anything you wanna tell me about Malik Palmer? That is your son, right? He was born on September 8th, 2010—if memory serves me correctly. And what puzzles me is that's around the time you proposed to me. How could you propose to me knowing you had a baby coming? Was that your way of covering up your fuck up?"

Leaning back in his seat, Aubrey folded his arms across his chest. "Well, since you have all the answers, ain't no need for me to open up my mouth."

"You're absolutely right. Since there's nothing for you to say, I'll just end this conversation. I'm done." I stood to leave and Aubrey quickly scrambled to his feet as well.

"I thought we was bigger than this," he said.

"So did I."

"So that's it?"

"I've heard enough and I've said enough. I'm done." Pulling away from him, I turned and headed towards the exit.

"Khari?" he called out. "Khari! I'm sorry! C'mon now, let's not do this shit. I'm begging you. Please…let's just talk."

I stopped in my tracks and turned to look at him with tears in my eyes. "I'm done talking. Right now, I just need some time."

8
KHARI

I wasn't expecting to return to a messy house. When I walked through the door there were was junk and toys all over the floor. The visit with Aubrey didn't go well and now I had to deal with a hardheaded son that acted like he didn't know how to clean up after himself.

"Sharon!" I called out. "Sharon, where are you?" I still had an attitude about the situation with Aubrey so I wasn't in the best of moods.

When she heard me calling out to her she came running downstairs. "Hey," she said out of breath. "I didn't expect you back so soon—"

"You had one job, Sharon. One job. I mean, come on. What do I pay you for?" I snapped. "To let Ali tear the damn house up whenever I'm gone? If you keep this up, I'll have no choice but to let you go."

Sharon needed the extra money for school, so I knew losing her job wasn't something she wanted. Her cheeks turned beet red in embarrassment. She wasn't used to me reprimanding her. Normally, I was pleased with her services but today she'd gotten lax.

"I—I'm sorry. He had a couple of his friends over, and I was gonna clean up but—"

I quickly realized that I was taking my

frustrations out on her. "No, no…it's okay. I'm sorry. It's just…I had a long day. My visit with Aubrey…Let's just say it didn't go so well."

"Wow, I'm sorry to hear that. I pray things get better."

Since I had nothing else to say, I fished inside my purse for my wallet. "Thanks again," I said, handing her the cash. "I'll call you when I need you."

"You don't want me to clean the mess—"

"No, don't worry about it. I got it."

Right about now I just wanted to be left alone. The shit with Aubrey had me so tense and stressed out. After Sharon left, I tucked Ali into bed and then disappeared inside the bathroom. Stripping naked, I turned the shower water on so that it was piping hot and climbed inside. I cried and cried and cried until it finally went cold and I had no choice but to turn it off.

Wrapping myself in a towel, I left out of the steamy room and headed to the bedroom. As soon as I walked in, I looked at the empty king size mattress. Prior to his arrest, we'd shared a bed almost every night—except for the days when he didn't come home. The days that he claimed to have spent the night at the studio because he was up all night working late—when really he was out cheating or laying up with Leah.

Now I began to put the missing pieces to the puzzle together. It all made sense now. Tears poured down my cheeks as I looked at the picture on the nightstand. It was a picture of me, Ali and Aubrey and had been taken two years ago at Disney World. Walking over to the nightstand, I turned the picture face down so that I wouldn't have to see his face.

Sadly, I was in too deep to walk away, knowing as much as I did...And Aubrey would never let me even if I tried to. After all, I had more dirt on him than the law.

Crawling into bed, I pulled the sheets over my body and cried softly. Our future was starting to look extremely bleak.

9
KYLIE

Purple reign, purple reign, purple reign...

I just need my need my girlfriend...

I just need my girlfriend...

I just need...

Purple reign, purple reign, purple reign...

I just need my girlfriend...

I just need my girlfriend...

I just need purple...

And I keep a pint of cup of purple like Whoopi...

And I keep the stainless steel on me like shoes...

They got me going way harder then we can't lose...

I had the conversation cause these ain't true...

I know you credit card frauds can't bust some moves...

I hope you're stacking money to the ceiling out the roof...

I hope you don't catch no feelings, for your bitch who fucked the crew...

Future's *"Purple Reign"* poured through the speakers in *Blue Flame Lounge.* The strip club was packed on a Tuesday. Me and Paige were making it hurricane in that bitch like we were rappers or A-list celebrities. We had bottles, cigars, Percocets, and towers of singles to blow through all night.

All of the dancers showed us love and the niggas *really* wanted to know who the fuck we were. Paige and I were killing the game in all-white. We were very presidential that night. Ever since Jamaal put the money in my hand, I thought I was untouchable. I flossed in the new car he bought me on a daily basis, I spent money like it grew on trees, and me and my girl celebrated every day like it was our birthday.

Half the time Jamaal couldn't keep up with me. I was too busy running the streets and having fun. He fucked up by giving me all that cash. A bitch didn't know how to act.

Me and my right hand were dressed like we should've been getting tipped. I was wearing the hell out of a white Alexander McQueen dress that hugged every curve on my body. My ass sat up right and commanded attention. On my feet were a pair of dark blue winged Giuseppe stiletto heels. The dark blue Chanel boy bag on my shoulder accentuated the fit perfectly.

Damn, these hoes couldn't fuck with me.

Just a few weeks ago I boosted for a living, now I was wearing all of the flyest shit without having to steal a single article of clothing. It was funny how quickly your life could change—and all because of some fake money that spent itself.

Speaking of which, I noticed we were running low on singles so I told Paige I was headed to the bar to re-up on some more. On the way there, I passed by a crowded VIP section that was lit with about twenty dancers and half as many niggas. They had that bitch smoked out too. There were bottles being popped and money flying around everywhere.

One of the guys gently grabbed my wrist to get my attention. He was fine, caramel-colored with amber eyes, thick lips, and a low cut fade with deep 360 waves. He had golds in his mouth and a couple tear drops tatted on his face. He was draped in all designer with a double Styrofoam cup of Purple Activist in his hand. He tried to pull me in his section too but I wasn't with it.

"Don't you already have enough bitches?" I asked him.

Placing his hand around my waist, he pulled me closer. "You absolutely right. It *is* too many bitches in here. Let's get up outta here then."

"And go where?"

"I'm quite sure we'll find something to get into."

"I don't even know your name."

"Terentino. But everybody calls me Tino. And yours?"

"Kylie."

"So where do we go from here, Kylie?"

"Damn. You don't beat around the bush, do you?"

"That's what I do. I cut to the chase."

"Well, how about I end it right here," I said before walking off.

***

I just pulled off the lot…

Two foreign bitches with me so it's only right I let my top drop down…

I just pulled off the lot…

With two bad bitches with me so I had to the let the top down because it's hot…

Rizzo and SosaMann's *"Off the Lot"* thumped through the subwoofers in my convertible. We were parked outside the Blue Flame, rolling up before we hit the next spot. Everyday me and my bitch partied from sunrise to sunset.

Paige had just finished twisting a burner when Tino left out of the club. He immediately walked over in our direction and I couldn't help wondering if he was preparing to try his hand a second time.

"Now you know I don't give up easy," Tino said.

Deep down inside, I was hoping he would say that.

"So this you right here?" he asked in reference to my vehicle. I could tell he was a car enthusiast.

"Yeah. You like it?"

He shrugged. "I could put you in something better."

"Well, like the old saying goes, actions speak louder than words," I told him.

"Shit, I'mma need your number before I can make anything happen."

"Where's your phone?"

Tino reached in his pocket and handed me his cell.

All of a sudden, his homeboy walked out of the building. "Man, I was lookin' all over the mufuckin' club and you out here fucking around."

"This *serious* bidness," Tino told him. "This ain't fucking around."

Hearing him say that made me raise an eyebrow. *Serious business*, huh? I liked the sound of that.

"How can I get in on the business?" his friend asked, walking up.

Tino looked over at Paige. "You heard him? Wassup?"

"Can't he talk for himself?"

"Yeah, I can talk for myself," he laughed. "My bad. I'm a rude gentleman." He was midnight black with smooth even skin, thick eyebrows, and dark wavy hair. "My name Touché. Wassup lil' mama?"

"Shit. Finna blow. I'm Paige."

"Nice to meet you, beautiful," Touché said.

"Well, shit, what ya'll finna get into?" Tino asked.

"Go somewhere. Have a couple cocktails. Get something to eat."

"Ya'll got room for two more?"

"Sure...why not?"

"Aight then. That's the move. We gon' follow ya'll." After exchanging numbers, he and Touché climbed into his 3 million-dollar money green Swedish sports car. Something told me he wasn't the average nigga.

10
CUE

After several long years, I was finally back in Atlanta—temporarily. Walking through the populated *Hartsfield-Jackson* airport, I reminisced on life before I left for New York. I thought about the woman I'd left behind, the friends, my father. It seemed like just yesterday I packed everything I owned and bounced. Fed up with the small town living, I went on to pursue bigger and better things.

After obtaining a master's degree from Columbia University, I became a successful entrepreneur and investor. Tackling everything from real estate to charitable organizations, to owning my own businesses, I was a young, black Warren Buffet in the making. And I always made sure that I looked the par.

On my way to ground transportation, I received flirtatious smiles from several beautiful women. They loved the sight of a handsome man in a three-piece Burberry suit and Italian loafers. I'd gotten my shoes polished at JFK so they were shining like they were brand new, right along with my Rolex and gold cufflinks.

The only things I had in my possession was a carry on Louis Vuitton rolling suitcase. Everything else was back at my condo in New York City. I figured I'd only be in town for a few days therefore I decided to pack light.

I'd just walked out the door when my phone buzzed, reminding me of an important business meeting that I had to cancel today. The reason why I was in Atlanta was far more important. When I stepped into the taxi line I noticed a familiar face at the front of the line. A smile pulled at my lips when I saw her.

Well, I'll be damned...

11

KYLIE

Looking and feeling like a million bucks, me and Paige walked through Lenox Square mall with new clothes, shoes, and Christmas presents for the family. We'd bought so much shit that I lost count of how much money we had had spent.

We had just walked past Fendi when I noticed someone pointing in our direction. It was the cashier from Nordstrom's and she was talking to mall security. My heart immediately dropped into my stomach. She must've recognized me and Paige from the other day.

"Paige, we need to get the fuck up outta here!" I told her. "Shit about to get hot!"

Paige looked over her shoulder and noticed he was headed right in our direction. His walkie-talkie was in his hand and I presumed he was calling for backup.

"Let's just keep walking," she said.

The security guard increased his pace and so did we. The minute he started speed-walking we took off running. Pushing people out of the way, we fought to get to the nearest exit before he reached us. In the distance, we heard him call for back up, and I was certain that we were going to jail that day.

Paige and I tore through the glass

revolving doors where valet was stationed. I could hear the officer hot on our heels. I thought we were goners when I noticed a familiar car parked in front of us. It was the same money green Koenisegg with embellished leather seats, and $16,000 black Novitec rims.

What were the odds of him being there right when I needed him?

Because Tino was on his phone, he didn't notice us immediately. Without a moment's notice, I hopped into his passenger seat like I belonged. Paige looked confused but quickly followed suite. "Damn, wassup?" he said, surprised to see me. "You good, you straight? 'Cuz you got trouble written all over you."

"Shit's hot right now! I need you to pull off!"

Not wasting any more time on small talk, Tino peeled off just as the mall security cop ran outside. "What was up with all that back there?" he asked, looking in the rearview mirror.

"I was in a situation that I had to get out of quick," I simply said.

"Well, I'm glad I was there for you. 'Cuz that's what I do, I handle situations."

I cut my eyes at him in curiosity. I couldn't help but to wonder what he meant by *handle situations*.

"So where you trying to get to?" he asked.

"I just need you to drop us off at my car. It's on the other side of the mall, where Macy's is."

"Aight, cool. Wassup for the night, since you ain't never hit a nigga up."

Before I could answer, Jamaal called me. He must've sensed that another man was in his territory. Now that he was back in my life he thought that he owned me but that wasn't the case—at least not for me anyway.

"Yeah?" I answered.

"*Yeah*? What the fuck you mean, yeah? Where you at?"

"I'm taking care of something. Let me hit you back in a minute." I hung up before he could say anything else.

Tino chuckled and shook his head. "Damn, ma. You savage," he said. "Fucking wit'chu, I gotta feeling you'll keep a nigga on his toes."

"I gotta feeling you can handle it..."

Tino smiled at me and licked his lips.

Suddenly, out the corner of my eye, I noticed that something wasn't right. "Wait a minute. This is where I parked! Where the fuck is my car?!"

***

Tino was nice enough to wait with us until Jamaal arrived at the mall. I didn't feel comfortable asking him to take me home so I told him my homeboy would instead. I wanted to call the police but Jamaal told me to hold off until he got there. I was so upset that I couldn't even think straight. Who the fuck stole cars from a public parking lot in broad daylight?

Ten minutes later, Jamaal pulled his Range next to Tino's sports car. I could see the look of disapproval on Jamaal's face before he even climbed out. He wasn't feeling the sight of me in another man's car.

"Aight, good lookin' foe. I got it from here though," Jamaal told Tino. He wanted to get rid of his ass as soon as possible.

Tino blatantly ignored him. "You good, ma?" he asked me.

"Yeah, I'm good. Thanks again, Tino. For everything."

"Alright then, I'll get wit'chu later."

Tino casually pulled off and Jamaal immediately went in on me. "What the fuck he mean he gon' get wit'chu later? So that's what you were taking care of? *That* bum ass nigga? That's why you had to call me back?" Jealousy emanated from Jamaal as he went on a rampage. "That broke ass nigga can't do shit for you!"

I just let him have his little fit since it was obvious he needed to vent. Deep down inside, Jamaal knew as well as I did, that Tino was caked up. He just felt threatened by the fact that a real nigga was in my presence.

"Are we gonna keep going back and forth or are we gonna try to get this whip back?"

I wasn't here for his ego trip. Jamaal had always been the jealous type.

Jamaal finally calmed down, ran a hand through his dreads, and sighed deeply. "I don't think we gon' be able to do that."

"Why not?"

"'Cuz I got the car from the chop shop," he finally admitted.

"WHAT?! That mothafucking car was stolen?! Are you serious?!" Now I understood why the car was gone. A tow truck must've picked it up while me and Paige were inside shopping our lives away. "What if we had gotten pulled over while we were driving? Did you think about that shit, Jamaal? Where the fuck was your mind at? You putting everybody at risk with your bullshit! I mean, at what point am I gonna be able to trust you?"

"Jamaal, man, you foul as fuck for that shit," Paige butted in. "You foul as fuck for that."

Jamaal had nothing to say in his defense. He was a con artist, a manipulator, and most of all, a liar, and he knew it. "Can't knock a mufucka for trying, damn."

"Man, just drop us off at Sahara Lounge," Paige said. "A bitch need to smoke some hookah and get her mind right after all this."

I couldn't have agreed more.

12
KYLIE

After hookah and cocktails, Paige and I parted ways for the night. I was ready to get back home, pop a Perc, and go to sleep and she was excited to meet up with Touché. They'd been kicking it heavy ever since they met at the strip club.

Tino and I hadn't gotten a chance to get as close because of Jamaal. He made it his mission to babysit me now that I had another man's attention. Jamaal wasn't the type to share anything—especially his woman.

When I finally reached the corner I lived on, I noticed Jamaal's Range parked in front of the crib. Young Thug's *"Power"* blasted from his subwoofers. He had the whole street vibrating.

This mothafucka is aggravating as fuck. Got damn.

I hadn't spoken to Jamaal since I went off on him at the mall, and to be honest I still needed some space. But it was obvious that he wasn't trying to give me any.

He knew he was dead ass wrong for having me and Paige riding around in that hot ass car. And he was even more foul for lying to me about it. As much as I hated to admit it, Jamaal would never change. He was a grown ass man now and still acting like the young ass thug I'd fallen in love with at 14.

Damn.

When will he ever grow up?

I was beginning to think it was impossible for someone like him to change. Every time I found myself having faith in him he gave me every reason not to.

"*Hmph.* Now that he done met Tino he wanna be all up my ass," I said to myself. Jamaal wasn't slick, and I knew he was feeling insecure now. Normally, he was the first one hollering he needed some time apart. But now that another man was on his turf, he felt the need to monitor me closely. Jamaal always did have trust issues.

After climbing out of the Uber, I slowly approached the driver's side of his truck. He was smoking on something heavy that had the whole block lit. When Jamaal spotted me in the side view mirror, he rolled his window down so that we could talk.

"You got a lot of nerve showing up after that shit you pulled," I said.

"Let a nigga make it up to you."

"Nah, Jamaal. It ain't nothing to talk about. Your bullshitting ass excuses have run thin."

"Fuck a mufuckin' excuse. I'm here to make shit right."

"Yeah, whatever," I said, rolling my eyes.

"Let's step in the crib for a minute." Jamaal climbed out the car and headed to the house. He was confident that he had me right where he wanted me.

I quickly stepped in front of Jamaal and reminded him how mama felt about us. "I don't know, Jamaal. You know mama don't want you around. She already told me you ain't invited to the Christmas party. I doubt she's gonna wanna see you in her house."

"I don't give a fuck about your mama. I'm trying to make shit happen wit'chu right now."

"Jamaal, c'mon, man." I tried to force him back to the car. "I'm not trying to get nothing started with my mom."

"See you always thinking a nigga trying to slide up in something. I was just trying to put you in something better. I know you pissed about that car shit. But fuck it. Let's take a ride."

"How you know I wanna ride with you?"

"You want another whip, right?"

My eyes lit up at the mention of a new car. "*Now* we have something to talk about."

13
KHARI

That weekend mama threw a surprise Christmas party and everyone in the family was invited. It would've been fine had she not enlisted me with the task of setting up and cooking. Since she didn't tell me about the celebration I wasn't prepared at all, but I still did my best to help out.

I didn't tell her about the fight I had with Aubrey, or that he had another family and other obligations. I still had trouble accepting it myself.

"Is everything okay?" Mama asked as I set the table. She noticed the gloomy look in my eyes and the fact that I was quieter than normal. "I can tell that something's bothering you."

All I wanted to do was curl up in a ball and cry. I didn't feel like being bothered with friends and relatives. I just wanted to drop off Ali and be left alone for a little while so I could clear my mind. I wasn't in the mood to party, but I knew how much mama needed the assistance so I came through. "No, mama. Everything's fine."

"Alright. When you're ready to talk I'm here for you." She wasn't buying the lie I gave her for a second.

Everyone who was anyone showed up that day with entrees, gifts, and bottles. When Kylie and Jamaal walked through the door together I did an automatic double-take, nearly giving myself whiplash.

So when did they link back up?

A wave of disappointment washed over me after remembering everything he'd done to her. I could never take a mothafucka back who did me the way he did her.

The Kool-Aid grin on Kylie's face suggested that all was forgiven. I didn't know if I was more upset about her being there with him or leaving me to help mama all on my own. The bitch lived here and was nowhere around to assist with the set up. And to make matters worse, she was here with this clown.

Kylie handed Ali his gift before hugging and kissing him. Afterwards, she made her way over towards me while Jamaal hung back to make a phone call. He was completely unaware of the evil glare mama was giving him. She wanted him there as much as I did.

Everyone knew about his bad reputation. He was a known crook, a scammer. You could look at him and tell he wasn't shit, but Kylie loved him like he was a perfect. *I can't believe this girl is really with this lame ass nigga.*

"Hey, sis!" Kylie sang.

"Hey, sis my ass! What the hell is he doing here? And where the heck were you when mama needed help with the set up? Out running the streets with that cornball?"

"Aw, c'mon now. You know I can't stay away from Jamaal too long."

"And you see where that got you last time," I reminded her. Kylie must've forgotten that he stole her money and left her pregnant with his baby. He was the type of man you would never put your trust in.

"Spare me the lecture, sis. Besides, it ain't my fault. Mama ain't tell me about the party 'til just a few hours ago. I had no idea about her plans."

I twisted my mouth and sucked my teeth. "Now, c'mon sis. You know mama told everybody about this party." Kylie was a terrible liar.

"Nice to see you too, Khari," Jamaal said sarcastically. He knew I wasn't fucking with him since I hadn't bothered speaking. Him and Kylie may've been on good terms but he was still a loser in my eyes.

"Don't flatter yourself," I retorted.

Before he could respond, I grabbed Kylie's wrist and pulled her away from Jamaal so that I could talk to her in private. "And when the hell did ya'll two reunite?"

"What can I say? Bad habits are hard to let go of."

"Well if you ask me, I think you should break that habit before it breaks you."

Kylie held up her hand. "Khari, please,

don't do it. 'Cuz you sounding real judgmental for a bitch that's engaged to a drug dealer! Aubrey ain't no better than Jamaal so don't try to act like you above the rest."

I quickly looked around to make sure mama wasn't in earshot. Kylie was loud enough for the entire Fulton County to hear. "Girl, keep your voice down."

"Keep your opinions to yourself."

"Fine," I said, tossing my hands up. "I will. But when he breaks your heart again—and believe me he will—don't come running to me."

"I never came running to you anyway. 'Cuz when things got out of hand I always went to mama."

Her insult hit me below the belt. I didn't appreciate her making me feel like she couldn't talk to me. As a matter of fact, I was downright hurt. "I don't get you at all, Kylie. If I didn't know any better, I'd think you like pain. Why keep dealing with a man that's only gonna pull you down?"

"You need to let me focus on Jamaal 'cuz you got enough to worry about...like that nigga locked down and that bitch that's claiming to be his. From the way it sounds, you got way bigger problems than me."

My jaw tightened after she reminded me of Leah. She was the only person I had confided to about the situation. And it was only because I needed someone to vent to. I didn't tell her for it to be thrown back up in my face.

I was just about to check her ass when I noticed a familiar face.

Oh my God...

Is that...who I think it is?

My heart started beating like crazy when I saw him. I felt butterflies in my tummy, and once again I was that same little girl with a crush. I didn't think it was possible for him to have this strong of an effect on me after all these years. What was it about him that made me so wide open?

"What's Cue doing here?" I asked Kylie in a hushed tone. Suddenly, our differences were placed on the backburner. Seeing him so unexpectedly was an instant distraction. It had been years since I last saw him. I almost didn't even recognize him—especially since he had cut his hair.

Rocking a navy blue blazer, white button down shirt, and gray slacks, Cue was just as handsome to me as the day I had met him. The all white Stan Smiths and eyeglasses he wore made him appear somewhat preppy. They were 18k gold, and although I knew that he didn't need them, they gave him a distinguished look.

Damn. He looks even better than I remember.

Cue dressed and carried himself like a professional. There was nothing street about him. He was proper, well-spoken, and articulate. There was a charming and suave quality about him that made him seem nothing short of a gentleman. To put it frank, he was the complete opposite of my fiancée.

It made me wonder if Cue and I had a chance had I never met Aubrey and he never moved to New York. I quickly dismissed the thoughts after I remembered that he was Starr's ex.

Kylie craned her neck to see him. "Oh my goodness, it *is* Cue. Oh my God. I ain't seen that nigga in a minute. What the hell is he doing here? And wait—*whattttt*? And he ain't got no bitch in his shadow either." She quickly looked back at me and smiled. "You better go jump on that, bitch. 'Cuz if I was you I'd be all over his dick. Speaking of which, Starr said he was hung like a stallion."

"Girl, stop! I don't need to hear all that. Besides, it's been years. I'm with Aubrey now. It ain't even that type of party no more."

"*Aubrey*? Girl, that candle been burned out," Kylie said. "You mean to tell me if he wasn't single, you wouldn't try to get on with him?

"I am over him—"

"Don't try to bullshit a bull-shitter. We're twins. I can feel when you're lying. I see it all over ya face—it's all in ya eyes. You ain't over that nigga. Hell, you haven't stopped fidgeting since he walked in."

After hearing her say that, I looked down at my hands and realized that I was. Kylie was right. Maybe I was still feeling some type of way about him after all these years. But we were adults now, things were different, and nothing was popping off between us. As far as I was concerned, Cue was nothing more than my cousin's ex-boyfriend.

When our mother walked by, I quickly stopped her to get to the bottom of things. "Mama, what is Constantine doing here?" I whispered.

Curving her lips into a sly grin, she gave me the side eye. "You don't *want* him here?" she asked with skepticism.

Her response shocked me. My mother was something else! All these years I thought she'd never known about me liking Cue but apparently she did. "I didn't say that. I just was wondering how he knew about the party. I mean, I only just found out about it this morning."

"Me and Lenny ran into Cue at the airport yesterday. He said he was in town for a few days so I decided to invite him. I figured ya'll could do some catching up. There's no harm in that. Right?" She winked at me before walking off to greet him and Cue handed her an expensive bottle of cognac as they hugged.

"*Unh-unh*. Lemme find out that mama a

messy Bessie!" Kylie laughed.

"Yeah, she real fishy for that," I agreed. If I didn't know any better, I'd think mama had an ulterior motive. She had never been particularly fond of Aubrey. Perhaps this was her way of playing matchmaker between Cue and I. Maybe she sensed he was the better man for me. They always said, a mother knew what was best for her child.

When me and Cue made eye contact, I completely froze up. I was so nervous about him being there that I had started sweating in uncomfortable places. Mama could've at least given me a heads up beforehand. Hell, we hadn't seen the man in almost eight years.

Thankfully, Starr wasn't in the mix, which made me think that she hadn't been invited. She and Starr weren't as close as they once were. We all heard about her setting niggas up with her new man and mama didn't approve. Starr barely even came around anymore. She was too busy in the streets.

My thoughts were interrupted when Cue walked up and greeted us with a smile and firm hugs. I could've been tripping but it seemed like he held me a bit longer than Kylie. Cue smelled of Tom Ford French Vanille. The scent was so intoxicating that I almost didn't want to let go.

"Damn, Re-run. Look at you. You're all grown up now, I see," he said, admiring my thick, shapely figure. "You look great." He stared at me like it was his first time seeing me and it made my heart beat even faster. It wasn't fair for this man to have so much control over me.

Making herself sparse, Kylie made up some excuse about helping mama with the food in order to give us some time alone. As soon as she walked off, I felt a wave of anxiety rush over me. Why did she have to leave me by myself with him? I felt like a shy, little girl all over again. It had been too long. So long that I'd forgotten the effect he had on me.

"So...um...how's New York?" I asked him.

Cue ran a manicured hand over his neat brush waves and smiled. "It's been great," he said. "Can't complain at all. I got my masters degree and picked up a few trades along the way."

"Cue, that's awesome! So what do you do?"

"Real estate development. I also own a few businesses."

An intelligent man with a career was such a turn on. And the fact that he was his own boss was an added bonus.

"Wow. I—Congratulations. That's great. It sounds like life is really treating you well."

"I definitely have to agree," he said. There was a natural air of confidence about him that I absolutely adored. "So what about you?" he asked. "What's new?"

"Well...I got my Bachelor's in Creative

Writing and English. I do freelancing here and there. You know, trying to keep busy."

"A writer, huh?" Cue rubbed his goatee and nodded his head in approval. "Interesting. We'll have to discuss literature over drinks sometime."

I wasn't sure but it sounded like an offer for a date. "That…um…sounds good. So…if you don't mind me asking, what made you leave Georgia in the first place?"

"I got tired of shredding papers and taking out the trash at my father's law firm. Don't get me wrong, he paid me well but…I just wanted more for my life. You know what I mean? I had to find my own niche."

"I know exactly what you mean."

Cue gave a dimpled smile and it made my heart skip a beat.

Clearing my throat, I quickly changed the subject. "Anyway, how's your dad?" Mama was his optometrist, so he was pretty close to the family as well.

Cue's smile slowly faded and he looked serious again. "Unfortunately, he recently passed. That's why I'm back in town…to oversee funeral arrangements."

"I'm so sorry to hear that. I had no idea."

"Not many do. He was sick for a while— pancreatic cancer. He didn't tell anyone about it. Not even me until recently."

I felt so bad for Cue. He was an only child so I could imagine how hard it must've been for him to deal with alone. "You have my sincerest condolences. He was a good man. If there's anything you need, just let me know."

"'Preciate it, Khari, I really do," he said. "But just being here right now is enough for me. Helps keep my mind clear."

I nodded my head in understanding because I could relate. Thankfully, the party was helping to keep my mind off Aubrey and his mess.

Suddenly, Ali ran through the house with the other kids while dribbling a soccer ball. He loved the sport and often bragged about how he'd one day be a professional player. I quickly got his attention so that I could introduce him to Cue. Ali looked annoyed that I was interrupting his play time but he quickly straightened up his face.

You know better than to be playing with that in the house. Now pick it up and come over here. I want you to meet a friend of the family, I signed to him.

Ali picked up the soccer ball and sluggishly walked over. You would've thought he was a teenager because of the rebellious way he acted. He was stubborn, just like his damn daddy.

"Cue, this is my son Ali."

Cue surprised me when he knelt down in front of him and proceeded to communicate through sign language. *My name is Constantine, but everyone calls me Cue. It's a real pleasure to meet you.*

Ali looked just as impressed as I did by his skills. I had no idea that Cue was fluent in sign language.

Cool name, Ali replied. *Nice to meet you too.* He then looked up at me with pleading eyes. "Anything else, mom?"

"No, go ahead back to playing with your cousins. But don't get too settled. The food's almost ready."

Ali took off running before I could even finish my sentence. Once he was gone, I turned my attention back to Cue. He just never ceased to amaze me. "Where'd you learn sign language?" I asked curiously.

"It was a pre-req in college. I studied it for two years," he said.

"Oh, okay. Cool."

"The little one…how old is he?"

"He'll be eight in June."

"So who's his dad?" he asked next.

"Umm…Let's not get into that right now. He's incarcerated and it's a long story."

"Well, I'm sorry to hear that."

"I'm sorry. I don't mean to come off brash…it's just…this whole situation has taken its toll on me."

"How much time does he have?"

"Nine years."

Cue whistled. "So what are your plans from here?"

"Well actually, I've just been taking things one day at a time."

"That's all you can do."

I wanted to change the subject, so I switched the topic to him. "So how about you? Do you have any children? Are there any little Cues running around?"

He laughed. "I wish."

"No Mrs.?" I asked next. However, I regretted it the moment it slipped from my lips. It wasn't my intentions to be too invasive. Cue's personal life wasn't any of my business.

He, on the other hand, didn't seem to mind my curiosity one bit. "No wife. No girlfriend. No significant other." He made sure all of the bases were covered.

"What? I find that so hard to believe."

"Why's that?" His eyes moved to my lips as he waited on an answer.

All of a sudden, I realized that we were standing underneath a mistletoe. How uncomfortably ironic? Donny Hathaway's "*This Christmas*" was playing through the built in Bluetooth speakers. Every year mama played it to death.

"I—I mean, you have so much going on for yourself. I just don't understand how you're single."

"Guess I'm waiting on the right one to come along and change that." There was a hint of flirtation in his tone.

Before I could respond, Starr and her beau walked in. Both were dressed extremely inappropriately considering the occasion. Starr had a short white dress on that practically showed the bottom of her ass cheeks. Someone should've reminded her that there'd be children present. And Shane looked no better with a red flag hanging out his back pocket.

So mama really did invite these jokers.

"Damn, auntie. Why I ain't get no invite?" Starr asked, loud and obnoxious, looking for attention. "I thought we was family. Damn. I had to find out through Instagram?"

Mama wasn't amused by her antics in the slightest. I didn't know why she was talking crazy to her to begin with. She wouldn't hesitate to put Starr in her place in a minute. "Because, Starr, usually when a person's not invited they're not supposed to show up."

Starr looked offended, but mama didn't bite her tongue for anyone.

"I'mma let ya'll hash that out while I grab

me a plate," Shane said before swaggering off.

Mama despised him more than she did Jamaal. In her opinion, we all had poor taste in men. She didn't like Aubrey, Jamaal or Shane.

Since mama didn't have anything else to say to Starr, she walked away with her arms folded. There was a smirk on Starr's face. She felt as if she'd won the battle.

Her eyes were glazed over and her nose was slightly red. She looked like she was on one. And based on her and Shane's behavior, they were already drunk.

"Who the hell put my dinner on Instagram?" Mama asked Kylie.

Suddenly, Starr looked over in our direction. "*Oh, heyyyyyyyy!* Cue is that you?" She didn't even bother speaking to me and we were cousins. "Damn, long time no see, stranger."

"I know. It's been a while. Nice to see you're doing...well."

Cue didn't want to make it obvious that he wasn't pleased with her approach or appearance. It was no secret that she had fallen off after he left. Starr had absolutely no morals or character about herself.

After exchanging polite hugs for old time's sake, they indulged in casual small talk. She was clearly happy to see him. So happy that she failed to ask me how I was doing. I mean, after all, we hadn't seen or spoken to each other in a couple of months.

All of a sudden, Shane walked up with two plates.

"Oh, hey, bay. Thanks," Starr said, reaching for one of them.

He quickly moved it away. "Hell nah, bitch. You better get your own."

"Boy, you need to stop. I'm trying to intro—Shane, this is Cue. Cue this is my dude Shane."

"Wus good, bruh?" Cue extended his hand.

Shane gave his hand an awkward look before finally shaking it. "Shit, boolin', fam."

"You introducing your ex to your future ex. How cute?" Kylie said, walking up. She loved to start shit with Starr anytime she saw her. She still couldn't get past their bad relationship. I doubted they'd ever be able to come to terms.

Shane gave a gold-fanged grin after hearing that. His eyes narrowed at Cue. "Oh…yo' ex, huh?" he asked, rubbing his chin.

"Yeah, but that was a thing of the past." Cue said casually.

"A good past, I might add," Starr cut in.

"The past, nonetheless," he stressed. Cue wanted to make it clear that shit was dead between them. And I couldn't help but feel like he was trying to prove a point to me.

14
STARR

Shane and I were parked a few houses down from my aunt's as we watched everyone head to their vehicles. The party had just ended and people were slowly filing out one by one. Her uppity ass thought she was being cute by not inviting me but I still had to pull up and grab a couple plates. I didn't know how they thought they could have a celebration without me anyway.

My aunt knew that I couldn't stand her or her crazy ass daughters. The only reason I put up with them from time to time was because they were the only real family I had left. Because of her drug addiction my mom was practically outcast. Her sister was the only one who stepped up to take care of me when child services intervened. Even though I didn't necessarily agree with her half the time, I still held a certain level of respect for her.

"Where the fuck that lame ass nigga come from? And when did you fuck with him?" There was jealousy all in Shane's tone.

"That was when I was young. That's why I ain't even go into all that. That's old shit."

"It ain't too old. You was smilin' all in the nigga's face and shit when I walked up."

"I was being cordial."

"Bitch, you was finna get your ass beat."

"C'mon now. We ain't gon' start this shit now, are we? 'Cuz that shit between me and Cue is done."

Shane watched as he walked Khari and Ali to their car. They seemed a little too chummy for my liking.

"You seen that nigga's wrist game?" Shane asked.

"What, his watch?"

"Mufucka had on an Audemars. I peeped it when the nigga shook my hand," Shane said. Because he was always scheming, he knew the value of everything; cars, jewelry, electronics, clothes, etc. That was his way of identifying who was worth robbing. "Them bitches run a quarter mil, easy."

I shrugged my shoulders like it was no big deal. I didn't see why Shane felt the need to broadcast that shit. I was still sour about the way Cue downplayed our relationship so I really didn't feel like talking about him.

This nigga straight tried to act like I never meant anything to him. He knows that he misses me. I don't even know why he's flexing.

On the real, Cue's standoffish attitude only turned me on. Seeing him again, and so unexpectedly, brought back all the old feelings I'd long buried. He still had a hold on me. We'd been together five years, so he wasn't just easy to forget. He was my first boyfriend, my first real love.

There was a time in my life when the nigga was my whole world. I loved him so much that I would've chosen him over God if it came to it. Cue had my mind, heart, body, and soul. I'd never forget the impact he had on me...but everything changed the moment he went away. Now he was back in town... looking better than ever.

"And? So what are you saying?" I asked Shane.

An evil grin spread across his face. His grip on the steering wheel tightened. "I'm saying that nigga gwopped up."

"He's always had paper. Shit, his daddy like this high profile lawyer. He works with all the celebrities and shit, and his mom acts in Broadway plays. Cue was born into money. That nigga always gone be gwopped up. What's your point?"

Shane's smile grew even wider. "My point is...we might have to pull a lick on that nigga."

15
KYLIE

Sunlight streamed through the blinds in my bedroom. Jamaal was sleeping naked, peacefully beside me. A pink Huracan Lamborghini was parked outside so he'd earned that privilege back. Although it was leased I didn't mind.

Wetting my fingers, I rubbed them over my pussy and proceeded to mount him. Jamaal groaned a little as I eased down onto his erection. Every day he woke up with a hard dick.

"*Mmm,*" he smiled. "Hey there…"

Biting my bottom lip, I grinned in pleasure. Jamaal had the perfect length and girth. "Hey," I moaned. My cheeks flushed as I rode him in slow motion. "How you feeling, baby?"

There was nothing greater than morning sex.

"Shit…better now," he said. "What about you? You good?" He licked his thumb and massaged my clit.

I swept my hair out of view so that he could see me. "Yeah…"

Jamaal grabbed my hips to steer me while pushing his own forward. He wanted to meet my every stroke. He never felt comfortable letting me do all the work.

"Unnh!"

A high-pitched whimper escaped even though I tried to keep the noise to a minimum. Jamaal pressed a finger against my lips. *"Ssh.* You don't wanna wake mom dukes."

Suddenly, his phone started ringing on the nightstand. He had forgot to put it on silent. So much for not waking up mama. She already didn't approve of me having overnight company.

"Who's that?" I asked him. I tried to look over his shoulder at the screen but he quickly ignored the call and turned his phone face down. He obviously didn't want me in his business.

"No one important," he told me. "Just keep doing what you doing."

I continued riding him until the phone interrupted us again. This time, it was vibrating. I was hella annoyed too because I was so close to cumming. "I guess it is important. They're calling back to back."

"Fuck that phone. This me and you right here." Jamaal turned me over and took control. Positioning himself behind me, he started punishing me from the back. I yelped out in pleasure when he slipped a finger in my asshole.

I was two seconds from busting when his phone rang again. "Since you won't tell me, I'll see for myself," I said, reaching for the phone.

Jamaal quickly grabbed it before I could.

"What the fuck wrong wit'chu, girl? Fuck wrong wit'chu grabbing a nigga's shit?" In a fit of rage, he climbed off the bed and proceeded to get dressed. That's when I knew it must've been a female. "Why you acting pussy? Lemme see your phone."

"I ain't acting pussy. It just ain't none of your business," he said. "Matter fact, I'll get wit'chu later." He didn't have too much of shit to say now that I was interrogating him.

Jamaal was just about to leave but I jumped in front of his ass. "A bitch call while we fucking and you think you just gon' leave? Nah, fuck that—"

"You don't know who it was! We ain't answer the mufuckin' phone!"

"Well, let me see then! Let me see for my mothafucking self." I tried to grab his phone but he mugged me hard as hell.

I crashed onto the mattress, and he went to leave, but I ran after him like a madwoman. When I went to grab his phone again he pushed me harder. "What good is it gon' do you to know? Whoever calling my phone is for me, not for you. What good is it gon' do for you to know?" he repeated.

"It's gon' do me some good 'cuz I'mma know who the fuck calling my mothafucking man!"

Jamaal paused for a minute. "You really wanna know? You really wanna know, bitch? It was my mufuckin' baby mama, that's who it was! Now fall the fuck back."

For a second, I simply sat there in shock and disbelief. I couldn't believe what the fuck he had just said. "What?! What the fuck you mean your baby mama?" I slapped him as hard as I could. "You trifling ass mothafucking stankin' bitch!" The tears were flowing before I could stop them.

Grabbing his face, I snatched his earring clean out of its hole, ripping his lobe straight down the middle. Splotches of blood dripped onto his tee. I had really fucked his shit up.

Jamaal mugged the hell out of me. "What the fuck is wrong wit'chu, bitch! What the fuck is wrong wit'cho mufuckin' crazy ass? I'm laying up fucking you and you worried about another bitch?"

"Nigga, you robbed me and ran off and got another hoe pregnant? That's why I'm acting crazy, bitch!" I tried to swing on him but he deflected my blow. Grabbing me by the neck, he slammed me against the nearest wall.

When I clawed at his hands he only squeezed tighter. Slamming me against the surface over and over, he kissed me every so often. "This what you want, bitch? Huh? This what you want?" He forced his tongue deeper in my mouth while squeezing tighter.

Tossing me onto the bed, he snatched his

clothes off and pinned me down like a predator attacking its prey. He had my legs pinned all the way to my ears, when he sunk his massive dick into my sopping pussy.

"*Aaaarrgghhh!*" I screamed out.

"Stop all that crying and take this big dick, bitch. All that fussing you was doing now you got what'chu want."

Jamaal was all in my guts as he talked shit. He had my pussy so wet and creamy that you'd never think we were arguing only seconds ago. He was the only nigga who could shut me up with the dick; the only nigga that made me cum the way that he did. His sex was my drug, my addiction. And he always used it to keep me in line.

"Them hoes ain't got shit on you," he said. "Kylie, you know you gon' always be my mufuckin' bitch."

16

KHARI

That morning, I was awakened by the annoying sound of my iPhone ringing. Rolling over in a bed that seemed entirely too big for one person, I grabbed it and looked at the screen.

Sighing deeply, I debated on whether or not I should answer. It was Aubrey, hitting me up from his burn out phone. I wasn't quite ready to deal with him yet but I knew eventually we had to talk. After all, he was my fiancé and the father of my child. I couldn't avoid him forever. Against my better judgment, I pressed the lime button and waited for him to speak.

"So you ready for me now?" he asked.

"Just say what you gotta say, Aubrey."

"I mean, I need to know…Are we good?"

"What do you think?"

"If we gon' be together, you gotta know how to work through shit. I mean, let a nigga explain before you tear a nigga down?"

"*Tear you down*? How the fuck you think I feel knowing you got a whole other family? How could you keep something like that from me? What happened to our partnership? Weren't you the one who said we were partners for life. What happened to our partnership?"

"Our partnership still remains as long as you let a mufucka handle what he gotta handle. We gon' be alright," he said confidently.

"I'm not gonna put too much faith in that."

"Then why don't you give me a chance to show you. How about that? Haven't I always taken care of you and Ali?"

"Just like you were taking care of another bitch and her child?"

"But did that affect us in any way?"

"Yes, it's affected us tremendously. You don't know how I've been these last few days. For goodness' sake, Ali has a brother he doesn't even know about."

"Well...shit'll work itself out over time."

"Is that the best you can come up with. Because I'm not feeling this shit at all, Aubrey. I'm not feeling this at all. As much shit as I've put up with, I *never* thought I'd have to deal with no bullshit like this! I mean, some things you can get past and some things you can't. And this is something I just can't get past!"

"Well, you know what? You need to holla at me when you can get past this shit," he said before hanging up.

17
CUE

Puffing on a cigar in my corner penthouse suite, I stared at the newspaper opened in front of me. Only my mind wasn't focused on the print. I was too busy thinking about Khari and how that ass looked in them jeans at the Christmas party. There was nothing sexier than a beautiful, full-bodied redbone.

She had that whole afro-centric, Neo-Soul look going on with the big, natural curly hair. She reminded me of a thicker Elle Varner. I found her whole style unique and attractive.

To be honest, I'd always thought she was cute even as a kid. I wasn't at all surprised that she'd blossomed into a gorgeous, elegant woman. So many people were going nowhere in life. It was refreshing to see a young lady with a career who was handling her business.

Such a rarity nowadays.

The last few women I'd dated couldn't even hold a candle to Khari. They had nothing going on and were only looking to be taken care of. Khari, on the other hand, had so much going for herself. She was career oriented, she was a fantastic mother. She seemed to have a very structured life and a strong head on her shoulders. I mean, what more could you ask for in a woman?

Suddenly, in that moment, I realized that I needed a break from the girls I usually encountered. I needed to switch my standards. I needed a woman like Khari.

The thought of her made me smile a little. She wasn't like the females I dealt with in the past. Khari was a good, wholesome girl, and I knew she wouldn't give me those same problems I was used to.

Ashing the cigar, I stood to my feet and walked over to the closet. Inside, all of my suits and designer shirts were hung and pre-pressed. I had stylists on my payroll who shopped for me and personally delivered clothes to whatever city I was in.

Pulling out a black Dolce and Gabbana three-piece suit, I looked it over to ensure that it was appropriate for my father's funeral. My mind should've been focused on that, but for some reason I just couldn't seem to stop thinking about Khari.

18

STARR

"Aye, you thought any more about what I said the other day?" Shane asked.

We were curled up together in bed at his trap. I knew what he was referring to but I still asked, "What are you talking about?"

"Bitch, you know what the fuck I'm talking about? That nigga you used to run with back in the day? Stop playing, man. I'm ready to make a move."

I hadn't put much thought into it when he asked me initially. Robbing Cue was something I was not ready to do. He wasn't just some guy I fucked in high school, he was my first love. We had history.

Sighing in frustration, I turned my back to Shane. He would never understand. "Yeah...I thought about it," I said in a low tone.

"And?" Shane pressed. He had an attitude because I was taking all day to come up with a response.

I didn't know why he was acting like he needed one all of a sudden. He already had his sights set on Cue. If he wanted to hit a lick on him he'd do it, whether or not he had my approval. "I don't know, Shane. Cue is like family."

"Man, that nigga ain't family. He just a

nigga you used to fuck. I'm yo' mufuckin' family," Shane proclaimed. "You sittin' here acting soft over some lame ass nigga you ain't seen in years. If I ain't know any better, I'd think you was still in love with that sucka—"

"I am *not* still in love with him!" I lied.

"Then prove it! Help me set him up," Shane said. "You said so yaself the nigga was gwopped up. Shit, this can be our biggest lick yet."

"Shane...I...I just don't know," I said doubtfully.

"So you gon' put that weak ass nigga over me?" Shane yelled. "Is that what the fuck you telling me?"

"*You* saying that. All I said was that I don't know. You're asking a lot of me."

"Bitch, we done hit licks on plenty niggas you fucked with. Now you acting brand new about this one?"

"Cue ain't just some nigga I fucked with, Shane. We were in a relationship for five years! Not to mention, we grew up together and know the same people. It would be hard to pull something off on him anyway. So many people know him...and so many people know me. We can't do that." I told him. "Everybody knows Cue."

Shane looked offended. "You think I give a fuck about that? Bitch, I know Jesus Christ but I still rob mufuckas."

"I'm dropping the subject..."

In a fit of rage, Shane jumped out the bed butt ass naked. Before I could ask him what his problem was, he snatched me up by my weave and punched me in the head. Bitch, you gon' do what the fuck I say when the fuck I say!"

I tried to hit him, but he held my hands together. Grabbing a wire hanger off the floor, he began brutally beating me all over my body.

"Shane, please! Shane, stop it! Shane, please!" I screamed at the top of my lungs. Every time the metal connected with my flesh it felt like a knife cutting my skin.

"Now bitch we gon' put this shit together! That's what we gon' mothafucking do!" Shane gave me a couple body shots to the rib. "We gotta understanding now, bitch?"

WHAM!

"Do we have a mufuckin' understanding?!"

"Yes, Shane, please!" I cried. "Please, Shane. Please...I love you, Shane."

Grabbing my titties, he sucked on my nipples like a starving newborn. "That's my mufuckin' bitch," he said calmly.

After snatching off my panties, he slid in between my thighs and forced his way inside me rather aggressively. Licking and nibbling on my neck, he proceeded to deep stroke me until my toes curled.

Shane was crazier than a mothafucka, but the man knew he could put it down in the bedroom. He had me sprung off the D; to the point where I wasn't going anywhere.

"You gon' do what the fuck I tell you?" he asked, tapping my G-Spot.

My ankles locked around each other, and my nails dug into his back. He was so deep in my stomach that I thought he might climb up in me. "God, Shane, yes! I love you!"

"You gon' help me make a move on that weak ass nigga?" He choked and kissed me as he waited on answer.

"Yes, baby. I'll do anything to keep you happy."

"That's what I'm talking about," he said. "You ride 'til *we* die."

19
KHARI

I couldn't believe that Aubrey had the damn nerve to cut the utilities off on me. He even had the car repossessed for failing to make payments. I guess in Aubrey's eyes there was a lesson to be learned.

As a well-connected man, he knew corporate people in every field so having my utilities shut off was simple. He wanted to remind me that he was the breadwinner, and that I needed him to survive. The mothafucka was sitting back, waiting for me to come at him humbly. Aubrey would go to extreme lengths to make sure that I saw things his way.

Sometimes I asked myself how I ever fell in love with such a petty, spiteful man. And then I remembered how much he finessed me. He always knew how to keep a smile on my face. He spoiled me and took care of his family. Ali and I never wanted or needed for anything. Most of the time, Aubrey was sweet, but there were moments when he could be quite the asshole. Like now, for instance.

To punish me was one thing but to make his son suffer was an all-time low. We had no gas, no cable, and no electricity. Aubrey was relentless.

Until I was able to get things back in order,

I decided to stay at my mother's. She knew something was wrong when I showed up but I didn't want to go into detail. Besides, she'd only say that she told me so and I wasn't trying to be lectured.

I knew what I'd signed up for when I accepted his proposal. I had to learn to take the bitter with the sweet.

After getting Ali settled in, I disappeared inside the kitchen to pour myself a shot of Louis the 13th. I barely took a sip before mama walked in and went off. "Girl, I know you ain't got my $3500 bottle of liquor in your hand that Cue bought me for Christmas!" She had a bonnet, robe on, and her finger in my face.

"You want me to pour it back in there?" I asked sarcastically.

"You already got it in the damn glass now!"

Grateful for her permission, I took a sip of the liquor and allowed it to wash away my sorrows.

Mama tilted her head to the side and looked at me as if she were reading me. "Is there anything you wanna talk about?"

20

CUE

The private memorial service was held at Northside Chapel funeral home in Alpharetta, Georgia with my father's closest friends and relatives in attendance. Because my mom didn't handle death very well she had decided to stay back in New York. Even though they hadn't been together in years him passing away had still taken its toll on her so she decided to grieve in solitude.

Among the attendees were Khari, Ali, Kylie, and their mother. I was very thankful that they showed up to pay their respects, and even more pleased with the beautiful poem Khari recited. I could tell that she put a lot of thought into each and every word. The fact that she took the time to write something special out of respect for my dad touched my heart. Hearing her speak of him made me think about all of the things I respected about him.

My father and I hadn't always saw eye to eye but I still admired him for what he stood for. He was an honest, forthright man who'd groomed me into becoming the person I was today. He'd taught me how to be strong, and how to be a responsible, and how to think logically. To put it simple, he taught me how to be a man.

Khari's words were so heartwarming and sincere that they almost brought tears to my eyes, and up until now I'd been doing my best to hold it all together. After the touching poem, Khari stepped down from the podium and walked over to give her condolences.

When she reached me, I pulled her in for a firm hug and whispered in her ear. "Thank you. That was beautiful."

She gave me a warm, sympathetic smile. "It was the least I could do."

She just didn't realize I needed a woman like her in my corner.

21

KYLIE

After the memorial service for Cue's father, I changed clothes and decided to link up with Tino since we hadn't talked in a minute. I needed to smoke after all that depressing ass shit and he always kept that Flocka on him.

I was solo at the Joystick Gamebar on Edgewood when he pulled up bumping E-40's "*Choices.*" His custom speakers were so loud they made the whole building rattle. You knew he was coming before he even arrived.

After Tino texted me to let me know he was outside, I walked out and climbed in his passenger seat. Everyone standing on the corner admired his flashy sports car. For him to be so low key, his whip always attracted a lot of attention. I couldn't help but wonder what he did for a living.

"Wus good?" Tino said. "What we got in our plans for the day?"

He was dressed casually in a red Puma jogging suit and a pair of white Nike Huaraches. A shiny, diamond cut grill sparkled in his mouth. Everything about his swag turned me on. He was sexy and his thuggish appeal turned me on all the way.

"I just needed to get away. I'm glad you came through," I said. "You wanna come inside or you wanna go somewhere else?"

"Yeah, I'mma come inside for a minute. You wanna blow on this loud stick real quick?" he offered.

"You know I do."

Tino fired up the L and handed it over to me. I pulled on it like it was the last blunt on earth. For a second, I forgot how potent his shit was until I started coughing and choking. Tino chuckled in amusement and shook his head.

Passing the blunt to him, he took several tokes. "So wassup with you and dude?"

"Let's not discuss him right now. I'm trying to enjoy myself."

"If you fucking with me, eventually we gon' have to."

"Well, until then, we just gon' take things one day at a time."

22
KHARI

I was surprised when Cue hit me up a few days after his father's memorial service. He claimed that he wanted to see me again before he left town. I didn't bother asking how he'd gotten my phone number.

I agreed to meet him later on that evening for drinks at Thrive, a popular restaurant lounge located in downtown Atlanta. I told him to give me an hour to get ready.

As I prepared for our rendezvous, I couldn't help feeling like this was my first date. I was anxious and jittery as if I'd never gone out with a man before. But Cue wasn't just some man.

A white crop top, royal blue midi skirt, and nude single sole heels was the outfit I decided upon. It was simple, sexy, and conservative. Doing something different with my hair for a change, I settled on pinning it up into a bun. Round cut diamond earrings and a few squirts of Chanel No. 5 were the final touches.

Cue had just pulled into the driveway when Ali passed by me on a hover board. I quickly got his attention. *Ali, put the hover board away and straighten up the house. I shouldn't have to keep telling you to clean up after yourself*, I told him.

Ali climbed off his brand new hover board

and dragged his feet to do what I'd asked of him. I started to tell him about himself until Cue rang the doorbell. When I opened the door for him my mouth practically hit the floor.

He was dressed to the nines in a Polo button down, black slacks, and black patent loafers with the bloody bottoms. He had a fresh cut, a sharp line up, and deep waves that left me sea sick. A platinum Patek Philippe watch glistened on his wrist along with the platinum diamond cut chain that matched his watch.

"Hey, Cue."

"Hey, Re-run."

I held my hand up before he could walk in. "We gon' stop this right here. Re-run is my childhood name. I'm a woman now."

Cue's eyes traveled the length of my body. "That you are..."

"Cue, is that you?" mama called out from behind. "Boy, get in here and gimme a hug!" she beckoned him inside.

As Cue passed by me, I caught a whiff of his Clive Christian cologne. He and mama exchanged hugs and casual small talk like they hadn't seen each other in years.

Suddenly, Ali walked up with pleading eyes. *Can I play the Wii U now*, he asked in sign language. He was addicted to *Just Dance 2016*.

"Go ahead and play it. But remember, 6:30

is dinner time," I told him. "Now gimme a kiss. And don't give mama a hard time either. Be good. I love you."

When I joined mama and Cue in the foyer they were still chatting. "Ma, please don't let Ali play the game past 6:30 because he has to have his dinner." I wanted to make sure that we were on the same page.

"You don't have to tell me that. I know when to feed my grandchild!" she sassed.

"Okay, ma. Just making sure you know our schedule."

Mama waved me off. "Girl, goodbye." She then turned towards Cue. "Alright, Cue now, it's always a pleasure seeing you. Ya'll have fun. Enjoy yourself."

"Okay, mama. We will."

***

Cue and I decided to have drinks at the Sundial restaurant in the Westin. The classy establishment offered great food and rotating panoramic views of the city. After we took our seats, he ordered us a $2500 bottle of vintage Dom Perignon. Subsequently, our waitress brought us bread and an assortment of cheeses.

Cue poured us each a generous amount of champagne. "I know I said it before but I really appreciate you speaking on behalf of my father," he said. "The poem you read really touched my heart. I'm sure father would've appreciated it as well."

"No worries. Really. It was my pleasure."

The waitress returned after giving us a few minutes to look over the menu. I ordered the crab cake and scallops and Cue had the black bean soup and prime rib.

"You know, Khari, something has been troubling me ever since we reconnected" he said once we were alone again.

"And what's that?"

"You never took me as a woman who'd be into street niggas."

"Well…you live and you learn…"

"That was well put," he said. "How's Ali taking things?"

"You know Ali. As long as he got his video games, electronics, and soccer he's fine."

"At some point in his life, he's gonna need a man to teach him how to be a man."

I was a bit offended by his statement. Last I checked, Ali already had a man in his life. "Could we change the subject?"

Cue picked up on my irritation and respectfully switched topics. "Absolutely," he agreed. "So I would love to see you when I'm back in town. We could make some things come to life."

I was blown away by his words. Was that

his way of saying he wanted us to date? "Do you really think that's a good idea? Because I'm not trying to complicate things."

"What's there to complicate? I'm single...you single..."

"Well, you know I haven't officially broken things off with Ali's father..."

"I thought you did, considering you're back at your mother's home."

I shook my head, embarrassed by that fact. "It's a long story..."

"We have time." He took a sip of his champagne. "Let's hear it."

23
KHARI

It was a little after midnight when Cue dropped me off at my mother's house. All of the lights were turned off and I wouldn't have been surprised if everyone was sleeping. Cue and I had gotten so wrapped up in conversation and old memories that I quickly lost track of the time.

It was so easy to talk to him. Until today, I didn't even realize just how much we had in common. Our way of thinking was similar and we shared mutual interests. I also loved how he showed interest in Ali. I really admired that.

He offered to take us to a major league soccer game but I told him I'd think about it. I didn't want to thrust another man on my son so suddenly. Besides, I knew Aubrey wouldn't approve of it.

After letting myself in mama's house, I kicked my heels off and reached for the light switch.

"Well, well, well. You finally decided to join us. Did you have a good time?"

"A wonderful time, mama. Thanks for asking. And thank you so much for keeping Ali as well."

"You know Ali's my baby. And he was no problem."

I knew she was lying. My son acted a fool whenever I wasn't around.

"I just finished making some hot cocoa. You wanna cup?"

"Nah, ma...I had a few glasses of Dom Perignon. I don't wanna mix the two."

"*Oh?* Dom Perignon. Mr. Fancy Schmancy," she teased. "Nothing but the best for his baby, huh?"

"You don't find it odd that Cue's interested in me after he's been with Starr?"

"Starr ain't right for *nobody's* son! I've been knowing Cue ever since he was a little boy. He's a good kid. I knew that he and Starr's relationship would've never amounted to anything. 'Cuz one thing about Starr...it's a motive behind everything she does. I know her, that's my niece," she said. "So if you two hit it off, so be it. The past is the past."

24
KHARI

Jesus is on the main line. Tell Him what you want...

Jesus is on the main line. Tell Him what you want...

Jesus is on the main line. Tell Him what you want...

You can call Him up and tell Him what you want...

The choir at Mt. Olive Baptist Church had everybody feeling the Holy Spirit. The place was filled to capacity for Sunday service. There were so many people in each pew that children had to lap up with their parents.

Me, mama, and Ali were two rows away from the alter. Because mama was friends with the pastor and his wife we were able to sit close— and not in the back where it was sweltering hot.

I was clapping my hands and singing along when mama tapped me and pointed towards the entrance. Cue had just walked in. He was polished and fresh to death in a gray two-piece Burberry suit. Everything about him screamed business executive.

Nice to see he's still a man of faith, I thought.

Growing up, Cue had attended church

every so often but he wasn't as dedicated as me. I donated regularly and helped them feed the homeless every month. There were times when I tried to get Aubrey involved too but he just couldn't seem to get into religion. Neither could my twin sister. Instead of attending church service with her family, she was too busy dancing with the devil.

Cue stood next to Deacon Ray while enjoying the choir's performance. After the service ended, mama met with the pastor's wife and Cue headed over in my direction.

"You look really beautiful. And I really enjoyed the service too, might I add."

"I didn't expect to see you here. It's nice of you to show up."

"You know I couldn't leave town without stopping by here."

Suddenly, Pam, one of the choir members, rushed over to introduce herself. She'd practically pushed me out of the way in order to make Cue's acquaintance. "Who's your friend, Khari?"

Cue extended his hand. "Constantine. And you are?"

"Pamela," she said, batting her eyelashes extra hard.

"Excuse me, Pam. We were having a conversation here," I politely said.

"Oh, I'm sorry," she said, in a syrupy voice.

"I just saw you standing here with this *fine* gentleman. I'd never seen him before so I thought I'd introduce myself."

Cue looked at me and smiled. "I'm sure you'll be seeing me around here again," he said.

25
AUBREY

That night, I decided to hit up my bitch. She had been ignoring my calls ever since I cut her ass off. She needed to learn what would happen when she fucked around with a nigga like me. And now that word had gotten to me that she was tramping around with some clown, I really had to teach her ass a lesson.

When I find out who that mothafucking clown is, I'mma bury that bitch.

I kept eyes and ears on Khari at all times. There was no move she made that I wasn't aware of. And the silly bitch should've known that the streets talked. I don't even know why she thought I wouldn't find out.

A mufucka like me had a lot of pull behind these prison walls. There wasn't shit that went on without me knowing. I had the streets and penitentiary on lock. The warden granted me special privileges since he was once a long time client of mine. The prisoners worked for me, the C.O.s were hustling for me, hell, even Leah played her part by smuggling in packages. I worked that bitch the hardest because I knew she'd do the things Khari never would.

I had everyone on my payroll. I may've been caged for nine more years but I was still living like the man. I had flat screen TVs, chefs that prepared gourmet meals, and an endless supply of imported cigars. This nine-year stretch would be a breeze.

Surprisingly, Khari answered the phone. I wasn't sure what made her pick up. Maybe she missed a nigga. My pops always said *absence makes the heart grow fonder.*

"Yes?" she said in a nonchalant tone.

"Yeah, I was just calling to check on you and my lil' dude...see how everything going."

"You know just how shit's going since you got everything cut off. We're back at mom's house, thanks to you."

"Well, have you had a chance to do that?"

"Do what?"

"Think about that shit you was saying last time we talked. 'Cuz that's a child. And I can't take him back, Khari. I mean, I tried to do right by you by not letting you know about him. I tried to protect you from this shit 'cuz I knew it would tear you apart."

"*Protect me*? If anything you help put the nail in the coffin."

"I mean, it was years ago...back when you went on that church retreat. I got lonely...And it was a one-night stand that turned into more than what it should've been."

"But don't you feel at some point you should've came to me and told me about Malik. I mean, dammit, Aubrey. The boy is five years old! When did you plan on telling me about him? When he was twenty-one?!"

"Actually, Khari...I planned on telling you about Malik before my bid was over."

"And that's supposed to cushion the blow?"

"Well, I hoping it would at least soften it..."

"Bye, Aubrey."

She was about to hang up but I quickly stopped her. "Wait a minute, Khari. Not so fast. I need to talk to you about some shit while you so quick to hang up the mufuckin' phone? Who the fuck is that nigga I been hearing you out in these streets with?"

"Excuse me?"

"Oh, we gon' play crazy now? You heard what the fuck what I said!" I yelled. "You gon' fuck around and get somebody opened the fuck up!"

"Aubrey, I can't talk to you when you're like this," she said before hanging up.

I tried calling her back but she sent my ass straight to voicemail. Knowing Khari, she had probably already blocked me.

"I CAN'T BELIEVE THIS MUFUCKIN' BITCH!" In a fit of rage, I knocked the chess board off table and began trashing my cell.

Suddenly, the door to my room opened. It

was rec time so prisoners were able to roam freely. Carmine peeked his head inside. "Aye, is everything straight?" he asked. He was a light-skinned pretty boy with soft, feminine features.

"Nah. You gon' make everything aight?" I asked, reaching for my dick.

Carmine anxiously rushed over to please me.

***

The next day was visitation. I wasn't expecting anyone to stop by and see me because neither Khari or Leah were on the schedule that day. Half the time, I didn't feel like being bothered with Leah and Khari just wasn't fucking with me.

I was surprised, however, when one of the C.O.'s informed me that someone was waiting for me. After dragging my ass out of the top bunk, I followed him down to the visits hall.

When I finally walked into the room, I was shocked to see the person who was awaiting my arrival.

It was my connect.

Taking a seat across from him, I clasped my hands together in front of me. "To what do I owe the pleasure?"

26
CUE

"First and foremost, how you feeling?"

"Shit, I'm maintaining," Aubrey said. "Especially since you got them ten years knocked off."

It was the least I could do, considering my personal ties to the judge. He was a close friend of my father's.

"I wanted to take some time to talk to you man to man," I told him.

"I thought everything was on the up and up," Aubrey said.

"Nah, I didn't come here for that."

No one had a clue that I was the plug. I kept my business separate from my personal life. That was how I stayed from under the radar...by moving in silence.

Aubrey became even more attentive after realizing I wasn't here for business. "Okay, man. I'm listening..."

"I'm glad you are..." I said. There was a long pause before I spoke again. "You know I've been hanging out with Khari lately. She and I seem to have taken off pretty well. I know you too have a child together...but I really could see myself having a life with them. After all, we did grow up together. So I'm coming to you like a man 'cuz I know shit's ringing off in the streets. 'Cuz when the streets talk, shit gets crossed up. And I don't want nothing to get crossed up between us. 'Cuz niggas lie, and bitches lie but numbers tell the mothafucking truth. And we gon' keep getting this money."

I had to come at him like a man after hearing all the petty shit he was doing to Khari—like shutting off her utilities. Even though I'd pulled a couple strings to have them turned back on, I was still bothered by him treating her that way. Now that I was back in the picture that type of shit wasn't going to fly. His time was up. Khari needed to be exposed to some real shit.

There was a sour expression on Aubrey's face. Crossing his arms, he leaned back in his chair. I expected him to come back with something ignorant. Instead, he simply said, "That's real talk."

***

After the visit with Aubrey, I swung by Khari mother's crib to let her know she could return home. Now that her utilities were back on, she no longer had to shack up with her mom.

It was a quarter after eight, when I pulled my Maybach into her driveway. Khari wasn't expecting me so I hoped she didn't mind me showing up unexpectedly. Turning off the engine, I climbed out and slowly made my way towards the house. As I approached the front door, I heard her mother's Angela Winbush records playing from outside.

Raising my fist, I pounded a few times and waited for someone to answer. Several seconds later, the door swung open and Khari appeared with a beautiful smile that made my heart melt.

"Hey, Cue. What are you doing here?" she asked, surprised to see me.

"Can we talk?"

Khari seemed a bit nervous at first but quickly got her bearings. "Uh—sure." Stepping to the side, she allowed me entrance.

After turning down the volume on the record player, we went to the family room to talk in private. Mama was singing "*Your Smile*" so loudly that we hardly could hear each other talk, so I closed the French doors.

"I just wanted to let you know that you could go back home now. Everything's all taken care of."

"You know you never cease to amaze me, Cue. You know you didn't have to do that."

"Nonsense. I wanted to. Besides, I couldn't leave here with you and Ali like that."

"Thank you, Cue. I...I don't know what to say. Thanks a lot," she said. "I really appreciate it...even though it's a bit much—"

"Let me be the one to decide when it's too much. Trust me, I'm not gon' take on more than I can handle…"

Gently grabbing her by the waist, I pulled her close and pressed my lips to hers. Surprisingly, Khari didn't put up a fight. Instead, she wrapped her arms around my neck and kissed me back. It was comforting to know she wanted me just as much as I wanted her. The moment I slipped her my tongue, the doors to the family room swung open.

Khari quickly backed away in embarrassment after Ali walked in. She didn't want him to see her locking lips with another man that wasn't his father. It would only confuse him.

In an attempt to break up the tension, I lifted my hand for a high five. "Wassup, man?"

Ali high fived me in return.

After engaging in brief small talk, Khari let him know that it was time to lay it down. "Come on, Ali. It's time to get you in the shower and ready for bed. It's already 9:00."

Ali dragged his feet on the way to the bathroom and I took that as my cue to bounce. I could already tell that she was having regrets.

27

KYLIE

Paige, Jamaal, and I had decided to fly out to Las Vegas that weekend in order to hit it big at the casino. After securing the largest penthouse suite at the MGM Grand, we all went downstairs to try our hands at blackjack.

Since I was the only one making money at the table, Jamaal and Paige left me to play Roulette. I was cleaning house, winning a shitload of chips, when security suddenly caught my attention. They were headed right in my direction with two police officers on either side of them.

Initially, I thought they were coming for someone else. But the closer they got, the more I started sweating nervously. When I looked around for Paige and Jamaal, I didn't see them anywhere in sight. Perhaps they had gone off to get more drinks.

Damn. Where the fuck are they?

Once I realized that I was about to be apprehended, I took off running as fast as I could. If they wanted me, they had to catch me first. I should've known the counterfeit money would eventually lead to this, but I was willing to take the risk for the reward.

Commotion broke out as they chased me through the casino. I was so determined to get away that I'd resorted to pushing and shoving people out of my path. I was almost to the exit doors when a burly security officer tackled me from the side.

Oomf!

I hit the floor so hard that I bust my mouth wide open, causing blood to pour down my chin and shirt. I could feel the gashes on my inner lip from where my teeth had cut into. Before I had a chance to say anything, they slapped the cuffs on me and read me my rights.

***

Once I was taken down to the Clark County Detention Center, I was charged with my first ever felony. If convicted of fraud, I could face up to twenty years in prison. For all of the shit I'd bought and all of the money I'd spent, none of it was worth my freedom.

After being processed through intake, I was given one free call to make. I wouldn't dare to reach out to Jamaal's trifling ass since he was the very reason I was in this situation. Paige crossed my mind but I doubted she had the money to bail me out. I thought about calling Khari but I knew she wouldn't come to rescue because she had told me time and time again to leave Jamaal alone. And mama was completely out of the question since I'd burned all my bridges with her.

With little to no options left, I decided to call the only person who I believed to be in my corner.

***

Tino had a bail bondsmen get me out a few days following my arrest. Because it was set at $50,000 they had to put down five-grand. After my release, I caught the first thing back to Atlanta, Georgia. Tino already had the ticket ready for me since he knew that I didn't have any real money. Although I was grateful for all his help, I was still pretty embarrassed about the whole situation.

One minute I was on top of the world, and then suddenly everything came crashing down around me. I should've never gotten involved with Jamaal and his crooked schemes. My sister always said he would eventually pull me down...and pull me down he did.

Now I had to hope and pray that I found a lawyer good enough to beat the case. I wasn't cut out for prison. I barely made it through a week in jail. I damn sure wouldn't last twenty years.

***

When I touched down in my city, the first place I stopped was Paige's apartment. Because I didn't have my phone, I wanted to get with her to inform her about everything that had happened. Not only that, but I needed to let her know how foul she was for leaving me stranded.

Paige shared a place out in Lithonia with her cousin who worked at Stonecrest Mall. It was a small two-bedroom apartment that wasn't in the most desirable location, but was very inexpensive.

When I pulled into the gated lot of her community, I noticed Jamaal's Range parked in front of her building. What the fuck is he doing over here? I know these bitches ain't leave me in Vegas just to lay up and screw behind my back. Paige was supposed to be with Touché and she was fucking Jamaal. Their actions were beyond foul and it hurt me to my core. I wouldn't have done what they did to me to my worst enemy. The shit was fucked up.

WHAM!

I punched the center of the steering wheel as hard as I could. I was ready to murder them over their betrayal. "Them dirty ass mothafuckas!" I screamed.

After parking, I jumped out the car mad as all hell. Blinded by rage, I slammed the door and rushed to her floor. As soon as I reached her door, I pressed my ear against it to see if I could hear anything. When I didn't, I covered the peephole with my finger and pounded on the door.

I waited for a while and Paige finally answered wearing Jamaal's t-shirt. The bitch was looking real comfy for someone screwing her best friend's man. Suddenly, and without warning, I hauled off and punched her dead in her fucking grill. Paige stumbled backwards and grabbed her face as blood gushed uncontrollably from her mouth. I gave her no time to recuperate as I started swinging on her like a savage beast.

"I trusted you, bitch! You were supposed to be my mothafucking friend!"

Suddenly, Jamaal ran out the bedroom, with his dick and balls exposed. To add insult to injury, he wasn't even wearing a condom. When he saw me mopping the floor with Paige, he tried to pull me off her.

WHAP!

I slapped the shit out of him, grabbed his balls and squeezed unmercifully.

Jamaal yelped in pain and punched me in the center of my face, giving Paige the upper hand. Using my disorientation to her advantage, she jumped on my back and started hitting me in the head.

Upon hearing all the ruckus, the neighbors came over to break up the altercation. I hadn't even noticed that I'd left the door wide open until now.

"You trifling as fuck, Jamaal!" I screamed. "You dead ass wrong! I can't believe I gave a lowlife nigga like you a second chance! That's all you fucking are—a lowlife! And you know what? Ya'll two bitches are meant for each other!" And with that, I left out of the apartment disgusted by what I had just discovered. One thing was for certain. I was officially done with both their asses.

What goes around comes around.

28
KHARI

I had purposely been avoiding Cue ever since our kiss because of the mixed feelings I was experiencing. On one hand, I was happy to finally have the interest of a man I'd wanted for so long. But on the other, I felt conflicted because I was still somewhat in love with Aubrey. Not to mention the history Cue shared with my cousin. Things were a mess. And as my attraction for him grew, they would only get messier.

I was deep in thought when I heard Future and Drake's "*I'm The Plug*" playing outside. When I looked through the window, I saw Cue parked in the driveway. To be honest, I was a bit annoyed that he'd popped up uninvited. Freely coming to see me at mama's crib was different, but showing up at my home was a whole other ball game.

Cue wasn't thinking about the position he was putting me in. All he cared about was the fact that he wanted me. Never mind the child that was involved. As much as I hated to admit it, dating him would only further complicate things.

As soon as Cue climbed out his Maybach, I opened the front door with an attitude. "You couldn't have called me before stopping over?" I asked with hands on hips.

"I could have," he said, once he reached me. "But I was hoping it wouldn't be a problem.

Besides, I wanted to talk to you. May I come in?"

If it wasn't for him being so charming and irresistible I might've refused. Stepping to the side, I hesitantly allowed him to enter. I knew that if Aubrey found out about me having another nigga in his crib I wouldn't hear the end of it.

"You're right," I told him. "We *do* need to talk." It was time I finally laid some things out on the table. "You can't just be popping up whenever you feel like it, Cue. What would Ali think seeing some man around all the time that he barely knows—"

"Khari...since I've been coming around, I've been watching Ali very closely and he reminds me so much of myself. I noticed he even has the same birthmark on his neck that I have." There was a no-nonsense expression on his face as he waited on a response. "I've held off for long enough...But I gotta know, Khari. Is he my son?"

Suddenly, flashbacks of us having sex in mama's basement at Kylie's baby shower came to mind. I could vividly recall the day like it'd happened yesterday. Cue was halfway up the staircase when he stopped mid-step, turned around and came back down. When he placed the cases of soda down and approached me it was as if my whole world had stopped.

Apparently, he'd known for years how I felt about him. He had somehow picked up on the signs and my body language. As a matter of fact, he was downright flattered by my attraction to him...and surprisingly, he felt some attraction towards me too.

After a few words were exchanged between us, one thing eventually led to another...

"You may've forgotten...but I haven't," he said, snapping me out of my thoughts.

Truthfully, I hadn't either. How could I ever forget my first time? Honestly, I'd just pushed it to the back of my mind out of guilt. He and Starr were still together when we slipped up and let that happen.

I felt like I was put on the spot, and I didn't appreciate him questioning the legitimacy of my son. "He's not yours," I finally admitted.

"How are you so sure?" he asked, doing the math in his head. I could tell that he was determined to get to the bottom of things.

"Because I know! I just know, okay! Ali is not your son. He is Aubrey's. And I don't ever wanna have this conversation again! Now I'm gonna have to ask you to leave. I've already got enough on my plate. I don't need this extra shit."

"Is that what I am to you?" he asked calmly. "Extra shit?"

"Right now, I just don't have room for more complications, Cue."

"My aim isn't to complicate things, Khari. I simply wanted the truth."

"And now you have it."

Cue just stared at me in silence as if he were trying to read me. "So that's it?"

"What else do you want?"

Cue gently grabbed me by the wrist and pulled me towards him. "I thought I had made that perfectly clear." He wanted me. That much was obvious.

"I...I just don't know, Cue. I don't think we—"

"Don't think about it then," he said, leaning down towards me. "That's the problem right there. You thinking too much." As soon as he made a move to kiss me I quickly stopped him.

"Cue...wait...don't..."

Respecting my wishes, he backed away.

"We shouldn't," I said.

"Tell me you don't feel anything for me, Khari. Tell me and I'll never bother you again."

I couldn't even fix my mouth up to lie because he knew as well as I did that wasn't the case. "Cue—"

"It's okay...I respect how you feel." With nothing left to say, he turned and walked out of the door. Little did I know, he had bigger problems than a wounded ego.

29
AUBREY

"*Trouble Man*" by Marvin Gaye was playing on the radio in my cell as I rested on the top bunk. I had a lot on my mind—like the mothafucka I had to deal with that crossed me in the streets.

Cue had a lot of gotdamn nerve showing up and staking his claim on Khari. She belonged to me. She would forever belong to me. Or at least that's what I told myself. But deep down inside, I knew there was no competition between me and a power figure like Cue. Hell, I got my product from him.

If Khari really was choosing, then I didn't stand a fucking chance. And since I was locked up, I didn't want to lose my support system or my girl—especially to another nigga. My family was all that I had. Who else would hold me down while I served a ten year bid? I needed Khari...more than she knew. I may've fronted like it was she who needed me but the truth was I couldn't survive without her.

In a cold, cruel world dominated by wealth, she was the only thing that offered me warmth. The only woman my heart beat for. The only girl that I loved.

Even though Leah had my son too and put in her fair share of work, I just didn't feel the same way about her as I did for Khari. She and Ali were my life. The whole reason for my existence.

Each and every morning that I climbed out of bed it was for them. I couldn't lose her to my connect. That shit just didn't sit right with me. I would kill a mothafucka before I sat back and let that happen.

Speaking of murder, I decided to hit up one of the killers on my payroll. Tino answered his phone on the third ring. There was a lot of noise and loud music in his background. Knowing him, he was probably at the barbershop shooting dice in the basement. He and Touché owned the shop as a front for tax purposes.

"Wus good?" Tino said.

"I need you to come see me. I gotta holla at'chu 'bout something," I told him. "And you know how these phones is. So we need to be face to face."

After Tino agreed to come during visiting hours, I hung up and began to put my plan into motion.

30
CUE

I'd just tossed back a shot of Jack when someone suddenly came knocking on my hotel room's door. A part of me hoped it was Khari, coming to make amends after the way we'd left things. My flight was tomorrow afternoon and I didn't feel right ending shit on a bad note. It was never my intentions to hurt or offend her. I only wanted the truth because I'd been wondering about it ever since I saw Ali for the first time.

There was an unexplainable connection I felt to him. We shared an unspoken bond that I couldn't quite make sense of. And now I was starting to think it was only because I wanted him to be my son.

If Khari insisted that he was Aubrey's, then I had no other choice but to believe her. I seriously doubted she'd lie to me and I couldn't say that I saw a resemblance between us. Ali was a spitting image of his mother.

Knock.

Knock.

Knock.

The person on the other end continued to hammer away, and their urgency made me think they were room service. Walking sluggishly to the door, I opened it and was greeted by the unexpected sight of my ex girlfriend in a three-quarter length pea coat.

Starr was the last person I expected to see. We hadn't spoken since the Christmas party at Kylie's home and she didn't bother showing up to my father's memorial service. As far as I was concerned, there was nothing to discuss, so I wasn't sure why she was even here. Then again, Starr had a bad habit of doing whatever the fuck she wanted. It was one of the main reasons why we never saw eye to eye.

Back when we were together, everyone assumed our relationship was perfect because I spoiled her and we always appeared happy. Little did they know we were living a lie. Starr was hell and her insecurities and flaws, intolerable. How I stayed with her for so long was still a mystery to me.

Starr gave an impish grin before biting her bottom lip. I knew what she was thinking before she even said it. "Can I come in?"

I figured she must've known someone who worked at the hotel. How else would she have found out which room I was in?

Against my better judgment, I let her inside and closed the door behind her. "Can I help you, Starr?" I asked.

All of a sudden, she snatched open her coat, revealing a skimpy, little lace lingerie set. I missed the touch of a woman and apparently my dick did too, seeing as how it immediately sprang to life.

"I don't know," she smiled. "Can you?"

"You sure you really wanna open that door again?" I asked, ever so calmly.

Starr responded by walking over, dropping to her knees, and unzipping my pants. Something told me to stop her but I stood there frozen in place, watching her pull my dick out before sliding it into her warm, wet mouth.

A low groan escaped my throat. Starr always knew how to polish a dick. Wrapping a handful of her hair around my fist, I fucked her face right there in the hotel room. I didn't bother giving her the heads up when I came because I wanted her to swallow every single drop. I even forced her head in place so that she didn't take off running to the bathroom to spit it out. Once I was sure that she'd gotten all her protein, I let her go and straightened up my pants. I felt regret as soon as it was over.

My heart just wasn't with her. I wasn't in love with Starr anymore. I yearned for another woman. "Okay now it's time for you to go. We shouldn't have done this. This shit shouldn't have happened." I was ready for her to leave faster than I had cum. To say that I was embarrassed would've been an understatement.

"Really, Cue? Really? You just gon' kick me out? C'mon now, don't be like that. We have history. You know that I still love you or else I wouldn't be here."

I wasn't trying to hear anything Starr had to say. Grabbing her up by the elbow, I practically dragged her to the door. "This shit shouldn't have gone down like this," I told her. "Look, I'm sorry but you gotta go."

Before she could say anything else, I put her ass out like garbage on trash day. It was time to leave the past behind me.

31

Unbeknownst to anyone, Leah continued to stalk Khari ever since she found out about her—even after their talk in Piedmont Park. What started out as a curious infatuation slowly transformed into pure and utter hatred.

Leah saw the way Aubrey had her living. It was a total step up from the tiny apartment he rented out for her and Malik. It was clear which family he was showing favoritism to, and Leah just wasn't feeling it.

It wasn't fair that Aubrey treated her like shit while she did everything under the sun to keep him on top. She even risked her freedom by smuggling narcotics into the prison for him. Before that, he had her trapping out the strip club. To put it frank, Aubrey was pimping her.

Leah felt like a total fool after realizing that she was nothing more than his flunky. Khari was the bread and butter and she was simply the water to wash it all down. Khari had everything she wanted; the beautiful home with the white picket fence, the engagement ring, and the heart of the man she loved unconditionally.

Khari had it all and Leah despised her because of it. So much so that she secretly planned on taking Khari out of the game...permanently.

This nigga working the fuck out of me but got her living comfortably while she doesn't even have to lift a finger. What type of shit is that, Leah asked herself every night? *Everything I do for this nigga and he chooses her over me! Well, I'm sick of it!*

Her jealousy eventually led her to do something she would soon regret.

***

The following morning, Khari's mother left out her home around 8 a.m. for work. She was driving her car that day since Khari had taken hers to get routine maintenance. She had an appointment with a client, and Khari promised to drop it off by the end of the day.

Mama didn't mind because Khari's car was newer and she actually liked riding around in it. After starting up the car, she headed straight to the nearest Dunkin Donuts for an iced coffee. It was a daily ritual of hers.

She quickly noticed that something was wrong at the very first red light she reached. She wasn't able to stop, no matter how hard she mashed her foot down onto the brakes. Mama didn't know it, but Leah had sabotaged the brakes in the middle of the night while she was asleep. She was so intent on causing destruction that she didn't even think about the child that could've possibly been hurt. Leah had no idea that Khari had swapped cars with her mother just before the sun rose.

All of a sudden, mama's car launched into

oncoming traffic. She tried her best to control the car but it was useless without the brake lines. Before she could get a handle on the vehicle, a sedan slammed right into the driver's side.

32
KYLIE

Tino was nice enough to let me stay in one of his empty cribs after the arrest and fight with Jamaal. I needed my space, and I didn't want him or Paige popping up on me at my mother's home. It was the perfect place for me to lay low until trial. I wasn't ready to deal with either one of them, and if I saw them I was guaranteed to lay hands on them again.

As always, Tino was out handling business so I had the whole place to myself. He never really came over much anyway unless it was to smoke, lay up, and rub on my ass while we watched TV. We'd only been kicking it a couple of weeks and we still hadn't fucked...not that a girl wasn't curious about it. Tino obviously was just taking his time with me. Besides, I knew a nigga like him wasn't pressed for pussy anyway.

I was in deep thought when my iPhone suddenly started ringing. I almost threw up in my fucking mouth when I saw Jamaal's name appear on the screen. *The nerve of this bum to hit me up.*

I thought about sending his ass straight to voicemail, but I owed it to myself to hear his sorry ass explanation. "What the fuck do you want, Jamaal?" I answered in a nasty tone.

"You."

His reply made me snort in disgust. "We all want things we can't have," I told him.

Jamaal sighed deeply into the receiver. I could hear the frustration and sorrow in his voice. "Look, Kylie that shit between me and Paige...We was just fucking around with that Molly, man. You already know what that molly make a mufucka do. It wasn't even supposed to go down like that. It'll never happen again."

"I know it won't 'cuz I'll never give you another chance to play me again."

"Kylie...please...a nigga been missin' you, man. I fucked up. Don't throw away everything we have for one lil' mistake. We bigger than that."

I paused as I listened carefully to what he was saying. He was trouble, and I knew he was trouble. But for some strange reason, I just couldn't seem to leave him alone no matter how hard I tried. Jamaal had a dangerous hold on me.

33
STARR

The plan had gone all wrong. I was supposed to finesse information out of Cue so that me and Shane could make a move on him. But evidently my emotions got the best of me. What started out as a simple visit ended with his dick in my mouth.

I was so embarrassed by what had taken place that I completely avoided Shane for the next few days. When I finally felt like I no longer could, I went to his trap where he chewed me out as soon as I walked through the door.

"Bitch, where the fuck you been?" he hollered, mushing me upside the head. "Who the fuck told you you could go MIA on a nigga?"

"Shane, don't start with me. You know I've been working on it."

"*And?*" he pressed.

"And...I don't think I can do it. I can't rob Cue..."

WHAP!

Shane punched me in the head after hearing that.

"Fuck you mean you ain't gon' do it?!"

"Bitch, have you lost yo' mind putting your hands on me?! If I don't wanna do the shit, then I just don't wanna do it!"

Shane slapped the shit out of me. "Bitch, you gon' do what the fuck I say when I say it!" He dragged me through the house and started roughing me up. In an attempt to escape, I fled to the bedroom and tried to slam the door in his face. Shane barged inside and knocked me onto the floor. He then kicked me in the ribs hard as fuck.

He was just about to kick me again when I grabbed the loaded pistol off his nightstand. Shane looked amused by my bravery. "You better put that fucking gun down, bitch. Ain't like you gon' use it." He didn't think I had it in me to pull the trigger. Sadly, he was mistaken.

POP!

34
KHARI

The sun was just beginning to set when I noticed Cue pulling into my driveway. I had told him that I needed time to think but apparently my time was up. I figured he had canceled his flight and secretly I was happy. I never wanted him to leave in the first place. But I also wasn't ready to let it all go for him. As much as I liked Cue, getting serious with him wasn't a risk I was willing to take.

As soon as he climbed out his car I opened the door. "I see you haven't left," I said with a slight grin.

Cue surprised me when he walked up and crushed his lips against mine. I had dreamed about this moment many times over; about him touching me, about him kissing me, about him fucking me.

"You know I couldn't stay away..." he breathed in my ear.

Lifting me into his arms bridal style, he carried me to the bedroom. Once inside, he gently placed me down on the mattress.

Cue mannishly snatched off my clothes, one by one. Afterwards, he undressed. Climbing into the bed with me, he positioned himself between my legs. I expected him to slide right in, but instead he slipped a finger inside me to see how tight I was. Apparently, it was to his liking seeing as how he sucked the juices clean off.

"You taste just as sweet as I imagined."

"Cue...*unhhh*...wait...what are we doing?" I moaned.

He curled his finger and tickled my spot, making me wetter by the second. I shivered and whimpered as he gently pinched and played with my clit. He had me so turned on that I soaked the bed sheets.

"Grab that dick," he instructed.

When I reached for it, I realized that it was much bigger than I had imagined. He was easily ten inches. I had no clue where he thought he was going to fit all of that.

"Put it in," he whispered.

I whimpered when he started rubbing the head against my clit. That shit drove me insane.

When I didn't move fast enough, Cue grabbed his dick and carefully pushed just the tip inside.

"*Oooohhh....*"

"*Ssh*. Open up for me, baby."

Cue teased me a little by sticking the head in, pulling it out and rubbing it against my clit. He did that a few times until I finally begged for him to fuck me. I was so wet and ready that I could no longer stand the foreplay. I couldn't wait another second.

Pushing my hips forward, I tried to meet his deep thrusts. "Don't play with me Cue. I need you," I cried out.

He kissed and sucked on my neck delicately. "I need you too, baby," he whispered.

Just when I thought I might cum from him doing that, he climbed down at my waist and buried his face in between my thighs.

"Oh, shit! Constantine!"

My back arched as his long tongue snaked in and out my honey pot. He skillfully used the tip to flick across my bud. He was an animal when it came to eating pussy.

Cue sucked, licked, and blew on my pussy until I shivered with my first orgasm. My walls always tightened after I came, but that didn't stop him stuffing his giant, horse dick back inside.

"Oh, shit, Cue!" I moaned. "We shouldn't be fucking like this without a condom."

He wrapped a hand around my throat and kissed me. "Fuck a condom. You gon' gimme a baby."

Cue pinned my legs forward, grabbed one of them and started sucking on each toe. With every stroke, my body opened up more to receive him. Cue was massive.

"*Unnnhh*! Oh, shit, Cue! Damn, baby, it's too much! *Ooooooh*!" I gasped.

"This your dick. You gotta learn to take it."

"This my dick?" I whimpered.

"This your dick, baby."

Cue continued to fuck me missionary position until I creamed all over his bare dick. "Shit, I'm cumming!" Tears filled my eyes from the pleasure he was creating. Before I knew it, I came a second and third time.

"You feel that?" he asked. "That's me owning this pussy. That's me making this mothafucka mine."

We were so wrapped up in the heat of the moment that we didn't hear the sound of two masked intruders entering my home. I had just confessed my love for Cue when I noticed them standing in the doorway of my bedroom.

A bloodcurdling scream rang out as I snatched the sheets around my bosom.

Cue jumped up in surprise. "What the fuck?!"

They quickly pointed their guns at him before he could make a move. I noticed that they each had silencers on them.

"Well…I'm sorry it had to end on a note like this…but your time is up," Tino said.

Touché cocked the hammer to his loaded gun.

"Do ya'll know who the fuck I am?" Cue asked angrily.

"A dead man," Touché said.

All of a sudden, they heard movement behind them.

In the blink of an eye, and without hesitation, Tino turned around and shot Ali in the chest at point blank range.

"*NOOOOOOO!*"

TO FIND OUT WHAT HAPPENS NEXT, PURCHASE YOUR COPY OF "I FELL IN LOVE WITH A REAL STREET THUG 2". NOW AVAILABLE ON AMAZON.

EXCERPT FROM "**GREEK AND FIONA**"'

1
FIONA

The African-owned lounge in Buckhead was more packed than a free Drake concert that night. I even thought I saw a few local celebrities sprinkled throughout. Damn. I had no idea Gunner knew so many people. It was my best friend's boyfriend's 23rd birthday, and he had the place jumping.

Trap music poured through the subwoofers in the dimly lit establishment. Everybody was popping bottles, smoking hookah, dancing, and having a good time. I almost started not to come out that night but I was glad I did.

A few of the fellas sized me and my girl, Tyler up the minute we walked in. As usual, I had to swat a couple of thirsty, drunk niggas away. Something told me not to wear the too-short BeBe skirt Tyler picked out at the mall, but she insisted. I felt like a fucking prostitute on GTA. Like the bottom of my ass was hanging out for the entire world to see.

Normally, I dressed more conservative: jeans, a crop top, and Chucks. I had a simple style—one my best friend constantly talked shit about. Tyler always said I had no sense of fashion.

Maybe it came from growing up with three brothers. I was a self-proclaimed tomboy, and Tyler had me all out my element that night.

Every few steps I took, I self-consciously tugged down on my skirt. My man would've flipped if he knew I was parading through nightclubs in this shit. I didn't even dress like this for him. The skirt was so short that I could feel a breeze on my lady parts.

Why did I let this broad talk me into wearing this, I asked myself repeatedly.

Tyler's outfit was no better. The jumpsuit she wore looked more like a cat suit, but with open cleavage. If it weren't for her bulging camel toe, you would've thought her outfit was painted on. Typical Tyler. For as long as I knew her, she dressed like she was on the set of a Gucci Mane video.

Tyler and I had been friends for years, but we were as different as night and day. Tyler was the life of the party. Tiny, feisty, and packed with a punch, she should've come with a warning label. Truth be told, she was the most exciting thing about my mundane life. I'd never been the type to throw caution to the wind like her, and I blamed that on being sheltered by middleclass parents.

Growing up, they never wanted me to be around girls like Tyler—which is probably why I stuck to her like glue now. She introduced me to a world of drug dealers, fast cash, and unrequited thug love. We lived two very different lives, but it was our obvious differences that fueled our friendship.

"Excuse me. Excuse me. Out my way. Coming through!"

Tyler pushed her way past the birds looking for their next come up. Gunner only hung with niggas who had money and drove foreign cars, so best believe the hoes were on standby. They easily outnumbered the men, but that was normal in Atlanta.

Tyler knew bitches would be at Gunner's neck, so she rushed here, barely missing a collision on the way. Gunner had a real problem keeping his dick in his pants based on what I heard from my girl. I was surprised there wasn't some desperate, pretty bimbo in his face right now.

"This bitch so packed you'd think they were giving away free bottles. Damn. It's hardly midnight. Do you see him, Fi?"

Even in heels, Tyler was too short to look over people's heads.

"No, not yet."

Tyler pointed excitedly in his direction. "Never mind. He's over there! I see him!" As usual, Gunner was dressed in all black down to his Balenciaga sneakers. Hugging his torso was a Helmut Lang graphic tee, and hanging off his waist were a pair of fitted designer jeans. Cuban link chains dangled loosely around his tattooed neck. Gunner was the most flamboyant nigga I knew, hands down.

Tyler gushed like a teenager with a school crush when she saw him, and I couldn't help wondering why I never felt that way with Chance.

We'd been together for almost two years, but my interest decreased after year one. I stuck with him though because he was my first real relationship. We met in college, shared similar interests, backgrounds, and ironically the same birthday. During our college days, he took care of all my school needs. Back then he used to be on his shit—now he was broke as fuck.

After graduation, we decided to move in together, which was a poor decision since he had yet to get a job. In the beginning, he would complain that he didn't want to work anywhere that wasn't in his specific field. I told him that was bullshit because beggars couldn't be choosers.

Chance refused to take my advice, and over time he just got lazy and accustomed to me paying all the bills. His ass wasn't shy either about fixing his mouth up to ask for money so he could party and drink with his friends.

On top of being jobless, Chance was also incredibly jealous and insecure. I guess since he knew he wasn't shit, he assumed I would find something better—someone I deserved.

Chance hated whenever I went out with Tyler because he always thought she might try to hook me up with one of Gunner's dopy boys. He didn't like me hanging with her either because, like my parents, he thought she was a bad influence. I didn't care about their opinions though. I was a grown ass woman and free to make my own choice in friends.

Speaking of the devil, Chance started blowing my phone up on the spot. I quickly sent his unemployed ass to voicemail without a second thought. He was probably mad that I blew him off to kick it with my girl. He'd get over it.

I would rather slit my wrists than have dinner with his bougie ass parents. His mother's rude and indirect insults always got under my skin. She never thought I was good enough for Chance—even though he was the one who didn't work. It was like she blamed me for his plight.

Tyler interrupted my thoughts when she took my hand and led me to Gunner's VIP section.

Since I took forever and a day to get ready, she hung back with me so we could come together. That was the only reason she was late to her own boyfriend's celebration. Call me snobby, but there was no way in hell I would've come on my own.

Gunner and I had a more fucked up chemistry than Tom and Jerry. Ever since Tyler started dating him we seemingly couldn't get along. He wasn't anything but a lying, cheating asshole. And to him, I was an uppity suburban girl with no sense of humor. Why the latter may have been true, that didn't change the fact that he was a piece of shit.

When Gunner saw us approaching, he quickly told his boys to make room. "Fuck out the way. Let my bitch through ya'll." Everything that came out his mouth was 'bitch this' and 'bitch that'. He called Tyler 'bitch' so much that I was surprised she hadn't forgotten her government name.

One time her six-year old nephew drew a picture in school, labeling each person in his immediate family. Every relative was marked accordingly *except* for Tyler. Scribbled underneath her stick-figure portrait in purple crayon was the word 'bitch.'

I always told Tyler that shit wasn't cool, but she claimed she loved it. I never understood Gunner's appeal, but to each is own.

Tyler and I had to squeeze past the collection of dope boys just to get to his section. Let Tyler tell it, he was well connected in the drug game, and his father was the Pablo Escobar of Africa. If it weren't for her, I wouldn't have known anything about this street shit.

Sparklers hung high above everyone's heads as waitresses fought through the masses to deliver bottles. If I didn't know any better I'd think the whole Atlanta was packed inside the lounge.

As soon as Tyler approached Gunner, he grabbed her ass and kissed her sloppily in the mouth. He wanted to make it known that she was his, in case any niggas with a wandering eye were curious about the chick in white.

At 4'10, Tyler was a gorgeous, petite girl with soft, mocha skin, pretty hazel eyes, and a coke bottle shape most females would pay for if they could afford. Her jet-black hair had a silky texture and reached just a little pass her shoulders. She was 100% African-American, but at first glance you might've thought she was Spanish. She made her living dancing full time at Treasure's Gentlemen's Club.

Gunner looked over at me with an impish grin. He knew that I couldn't stand his mothafucking ass. Every week, Tyler came crying to me about the foul shit Gunner put her through. Between the cheating and the abuse, I didn't know what she saw in the fool other than his looks.

"Freakazoid, wus good? Glad yo' nigga let you off the leash long enough to come through."

I ignored Gunner's rude comment and pretended to be interested in my surroundings. I *was* gonna tell him happy birthday, but he ruined any chances of me being cordial.

He called me any silly ass name he could think of because of the white section of hair in the front of my head. I inherited the birthmark from my father and was stuck with it for life. I used to dye it black occasionally, but it came back on its own so quickly that I just gave up on it.

"Aye, leave my girl alone," Tyler laughed, coming to my defense. "Don't start tonight." Gunner and me were like Pam and Martin. Every time we saw one another, shots were fired.

"Man, I'm just fuckin' with that bitch. Chill."

Gunner looked at me and smiled, revealing his gold bottom grill. I swear that nigga made my ass itch.

"C'mon Fiona, lighten up. Have a drink with me for my birthday!"

Gunner held out a white Styrofoam cup and I frowned. Knowing him, it most likely wasn't fruit punch. "I have a feeling I don't want what ya'll sipping."

Gunner was about to hit me with some smart-mouthed comeback, but something else caught his attention. "Aye, my mufuckin' brotha in this bitch!" he said excitedly. Everyone turned his or her attention to his sibling.

Subconsciously, I turned as well and saw the sexiest man I'd ever laid eyes on in my 21 years. At 6'2, Gunner's brother had a lean and muscular physique. He was dark-skinned; the color of melted cocoa. Long lashes that curled upward shielded his big, bright eyes. There was a calm look on his chiseled face. A boss-like presence could be felt as soon as he walked into the room.

Hoes' heads swiveled in curiosity. Gunner's brother oozed money, and every gold-digger in a 20-mile radius sensed it. Dressed in a three-piece Dolce and Gabbana suit, he looked like he was some big league business executive. Like he worked on Wall Street or something. The diamond cufflinks around his wrist sparkled, and on his feet was a pair cognac-colored Gucci loafers. The only jewelry he donned was a pristine platinum Rolex. His baldhead shined under the spot light in the lounge. He was polished, assertive, and fine as hell.

Damn. *That's* his brother?

His lips and dimples were by far my favorite feature. I shouldn't have been looking so closely, but I couldn't help myself.

"Damn, bitch. If you gon' stare that hard you may as well say hi," Tyler whispered in my ear.

"What makes you think I want his brother?"

"I didn't say you wanted his brother, you did," she said. "So do you?"

"Do I what?"

"Want his brother?" she asked. "If you do, I can pass the word on—"

"Girl, stop it. So I could end up with a nigga like Gunner? No thanks. I don't need that fucking headache. Plus, I already got a man in case you forgot."

"Bitch, you been ignoring that nigga's calls all night. Looks to me like *you* the one who forgot about his ass."

I didn't have a response for her solid accusation. I was saying one thing, but in reality, I was in fact curious about Gunner's brother. I had a feeling he was nothing like his younger sibling. With his poise and formal attire, he looked unquestionably mature.

I was in a complete state of hypnosis before Gunner pushed past me and spilled his drink all over my expensive skirt. He didn't even apologize as he ran up to his brother and hugged him.

I cut my eyes at Tyler in anger and she gave a look that said 'be nice.' I wasn't trying to hear that. I wanted to kill him, and apart of me thought he did that shit on purpose. "Girl, I'mma have to go to the ladies room and get myself together. I can't walk around like this. I'll be back." Walking off in a huff, I headed to the restroom. That shit just totally blew my night.

As I walked past Gunner, his brother and me locked gazes. He was even sexier up close in person.

Did he come alone? Surprisingly, there wasn't a woman on his arm. Every single chick in the place had her eyes on him so I was sure that wouldn't last long.

Dozens of questions ran through my mind, as if I didn't already have a boyfriend at home.

Me and Gunner's brother continued to take in each other's appearance. The curt smirk he gave showed that he was appreciative of what he saw. The feeling was undoubtedly mutual.

We stared at each other so long that I wound up bumping into Tyler's twin sister, Skyler.

"Damn, Fiona. Watch where you going!" she snapped.

Skyler and me were never cool per se, but we were cordial for the most part. I don't know why she didn't like me, and quite honestly I didn't care. After mumbling a quick apology, I rushed off to the bathroom before I was further embarrassed.

EXCERPT FROM "**YOUR SPOUSE, MY SPONSOR**"

Seventeen-year old Kirby Caldwell multi-tasked between carrying a tray of food and drinks to the table of fine ass men straight ahead. Judging from their swagger and poise, they didn't look like they were from Philly. Couldn't be. The European designer clothing, shiny jewelry, and expensive cologne screamed foreign. Kirby was drawn to them instantly like moths to a flame. The boys she saw on an everyday basis were certainly not of their caliber.

These niggas are the real deal. Ever since they walked in, Kirby had been wracking her brain about what they did for a living. They were far from being the blue-collar type. They had trouble written all over, but for some reason she was still drawn to them.

Maybe they're staying upstairs in the Windsor suites, Kirby thought to herself. The customers at the pub she worked at were mainly guests who took advantage of the discount offered by the hotel.

As soon as Kirby reached their table, she pushed her thoughts to the back of her mind. All four men were in deep in conversation prior to her arrival but stopped the minute she approached them.

Kirby felt odd as each man sized her up. It made her nervous, because she knew they were trying to decide if they appreciated what they saw. She was thin with A-cup breasts, small hips, and an ass she thought was too big for her tiny frame. In her opinion Kirby thought she was just average. Nothing special, but nothing too bad to look at. One of her admirers, on the other hand, held an entirely different sentiment.

"Aye, you got a tough lil' body on you, ma. That thing pokin' too. How old is you, if you don't mind me askin'?" Aviance's eyes traveled the length of Kirby's petite body. He loved a skinny bitch with a fat ass. Someone he could easily manhandle while sticking the pipe to.

At only 20, he was the most flamboyant of the quartet. They were only politicking over dinner, and the nigga had on two diamond chains and a sparkling diamond grill. If it weren't for the fact that he kept a shooter 'round him, he would've been robbed countless times.

Aviance was damn near blinding everyone in the establishment, but he loved showing off. He also loved gorgeous women, and never bit his tongue when it came to expressing it. A smirk pulled at his full lips as he admired what he saw. Kirby was definitely his type. He was just about to go in for the kill when his boss cut in.

"Ease up, bruh. Swear yo' ass don't know how to act whenever you see a bad bitch. My bad, you gotta excuse my nephew."

After hearing the word 'bitch', Kirby did an automatic double take. She started to check his ass when suddenly she noticed how fine he was. She damn near spilled the drinks looking.

Smooth midnight black skin, pearl white teeth, chiseled jawline, and muscular build. *Gotdamn.* He looked like an African king—like the tribal warriors she read about in her black History books. He was beautiful.

Castle looked every bit of the boss he was in a black Givenchy tee and black high top Giuseppes. A black and gray Louis Vuitton belt secured his tan designer jeans. He had $120,000 on his wrist like money grew on trees.

I bet his ass got a flock of hoes at his beck and call though, Kirby presumed. Although she told herself that, she tampered with the thought of possibly being one of them. It must've been nice. She then laughed inside after realizing how out of her league he was. There he sat, draped in expensive clothes and jewelry while she waited on tables.

Kirby imagined him only dating Beyonces and Rihannas anyway. *I got as much chance ending up with him as I do hitting the lottery*, she told herself. *Keep dreaming.*

Nervously clearing her throat, Kirby placed the dishes in their respectable places and rushed off before she embarrassed herself. Her best friend, McKenzie was patiently awaiting her arrival behind the bar. She, too, was a waitress at the pub they worked at. The quaint mom and pop restaurant didn't get much business other than that of hotel guests, so they stood around talking shit all day until it was time to clock out.

"Girl, I'm so fucking jealous. I was praying I got their section," McKenzie joked. "Them jawns fine as shit, ain't they. And that dark-skinned one could get the mothafucking business. I'm just saying." She had a weakness for chocolate men.

Although Kirby and McKenzie were like sisters, they were as different as night and day. At 18, McKenzie was a tall, slender redbone with mint green eyes, freckles, and reddish brown hair that she inherited from her white daddy. He had walked out on her when she was just two-years old. This was after his wife found out about his sidepiece. McKenzie was a product of messiness. She was also very promiscuous.

Sometimes Kirby wondered if she was that way because of what her father did. Kirby reserved her judgment since they were girls despite her mother's constant warnings about the company she kept. She had never really cared for McKenzie.

"I'm not gonna lie, they low-key had me nervous. I wish you had gotten their section too. I dread having to go back over there," Kirby laughed.

"Damn, Kirbz, you gotta stop acting so scared of niggas. I swear, every time you get in the presence of a dude you retreat—"

"Bullshit," Kirby argued.

"Bitch, you practically ran from that section," McKenzie reminded her. "Besides, name the last time you even dealt with a nigga...and kindergarten don't count—"

"Don't come for me, sweetie. I told you I dry pumped in the girl's bathroom once and you won't let that shit go," Kirby laughed.

"Bitch, that was your best and *only* experience," her friend teased. "You need to get you some real dick, and quit acting so timid." McKenzie often teased her friend about her virgin status.

"Don't try to come down on me just 'cuz my track record don't match yours. When I'm ready I will."

Instead of entertaining Kirby's low blow, McKenzie pointed back to the fellas' table. "*Ooh*, look. One of 'em still checking you out," she giggled. "That mothafucka is too damn fine. What'd you do to that man, bish?"

Kirby was almost scared to crane her neck. "Girl, quit playing. I haven't done anything." When she finally turned to look she noticed Castle staring directly at her. Kirby didn't know it yet, but he had already staked his claim on the young woman.

***

Since Kirby's shift ended three hours before McKenzie's she wound up catching the bus alone. Once she was let off at her stop, she walked the rest of the way. The routine had become as normal as breathing. South Philly wasn't exactly a safe haven, but she'd been living there all her life.

Kirby often dreamt about the day she was able to move out the hood and buy her first whip. She already knew what she wanted: a pearl white Mercedes Benz with shiny chrome rims. Instead of saving up for her dream car, Kirby had to pay utility and hospital bills. Three years ago her mom, Leah lost her left breast to cancer. It went in remission for a little while, but was now back and more aggressive than ever. Leah's heaping medical expenses left them bankrupt. The government assistance helped out some, but it wasn't nearly enough to support a dying woman and her teenage children.

Kirby's brother, Kaleb was a year older than her and stayed in and out of jail. He'd done everything from robbing to stealing in order to provide for his family—but the law eventually caught up with him.

It had been two years since the police kicked her door off the hinges to apprehend him. They dragged Kaleb off faster than they were able to read his Miranda rights. He was only seventeen at the time. They charged him for stealing and flipping cars, and he was left to rot in a human zoo.

In the beginning, Kaleb used to write his sister religiously, but over time his communication eventually slowed down. She figured he might've just wanted to serve his time in solitude. Though Kirby missed him, she wouldn't dare become a burden. She didn't know what he was going through alone in prison, but she didn't want to add more to his plate with her troubles. Kirby figured the least she could do was take care of mom and hold things down until he was released—whenever that was.

All of a sudden, the light blaring of a horn interrupted Kirby's thoughts. She noticed a shiny black Rolls Royce ease alongside her. The driver of the fancy vehicle made sure to match his pace with her walking.

"Aye, why you out here walkin' alone, mama. You need a ride or somethin'?"

Kirby recognized the voice before she did the driver. Seeing him again, and so unexpectedly, made her nervous. He made her palms sweat and her stomach flip-flop. *Damn.* What was it about him that made her get butterflies and fall apart whenever she was in his presence? What the hell was he doing in her hood anyway?

Kirby looked around to make sure he wasn't talking to someone else. It seemed almost impossible for him to show an interest in her. Someone who was flat-chested and average at best. She wondered if he was fucking with her for the hell of it. It would've been a crude thing to do if he was.

Just keep walking.

Kirby told herself one thing, but her curiosity outweighed her common sense.

"Aye, don't act like you don't see me." The hint of humor in his tone was enough to let her know he wasn't too serious. "I ain't from 'round here but I know it ain't safe for a young lady to be walkin' alone. C'mon. I ain't gon' bite." Castle brought his car to a slow stop, reached over and opened the passenger door.

He was in Philly for business purposes, but on that side of town to visit one of his freaks—a badass stripper he'd met at *Onyx*. He was on his way to her crib when he saw something more promising from the corner of his eye. Nothing intrigued him more than the prospect of new pussy, so he did what any self-righteous nigga would. He pulled up on her ass.

Ironically, before he left the restaurant with his boys, Castle passed his number to McKenzie to give to Kirby who was in the restroom at the time. What he didn't know was that McKenzie had jealously ripped it up and tossed it out. On the low, she was mad he hadn't hollered at her first. She'd been checking for him too; she peeped Castle the minute he walked in, but it was obvious whom he was more interested in. Naturally, McKenzie wasn't feeling that shit. In her world, no man would choose Kirby over her.

McKenzie believed cute light-skinned girls reigned supreme.

Unfortunately, she had no control over fate and pure coincidence. Somehow Castle and Kirby still ended up bumping into each other.

Kirby cautiously peered inside his ride to verify he was by himself. *I probably shouldn't*, she told herself. She had never actually climbed in the car with a total stranger before. Since a young girl she knew better than to ever do something so stupid. Kirby knew what she should've done. She should have continued walking...but her legs had a mind of their own as they slowly approached his flashy car.

"Is it...safe?" Kirby asked shyly. Castle made her unashamedly bashful, and he knew it was because he intimidated her. Men of his caliber didn't speak to chicks like her. Hell, they barely even gave them a second look. Castle found her nervous demeanor cute.

Chuckling at her innocent question, he asked, "How old are you, baby girl?"

"...Seventeen."

Castle refused to tell her that he had a daughter a year younger than her. "Aye, look. You in good hands, lil' mama. I promise."

Kirby slowly climbed inside, sealing her fate as soon as she closed the door. She figured there was no harm in allowing him to take her home. Besides, it wasn't like she didn't find him attractive.

"Why's it so fuckin' dark in this city? Like damn. Tax money won't cover the cost of some streetlights 'round dis mufucka? Gotta feel like you walkin' through the 'hood blind folded or some shit. You be walkin' every day at this time?"

"Yeah, but usually I'm with my girl McKenzie. We work together and she stays a block from me."

"Oh, nah. You too damn pretty to be on foot," he said, shaking his head. "If you was my bitch, I wouldn't have yo' ass walkin'."

Wale's new album played softly through his custom speakers. His interior smelled of Clive Christian cologne and top quality loud. Kirby didn't smoke, but she was familiar with the scent because Kaleb once sold it. That boy had damn near done everything under the sun just to put food in the fridge. He'd sacrificed his freedom to take care of her and their mom.

"What's yo' address?" Castle asked.

Kirby rattled off where she lived before fastening her seatbelt. She shouldn't have been so comfortable with him, but for some reason she felt like she could trust him.

After plugging her address in his GPS, he retrieved the L tucked behind his ear. He'd dropped several stacks to have a police monitor installed so that he could track how close a squad car was. Twelve loved to fuck with a nigga with some paper.

"You chief?" Castle asked, holding up the blunt.

"No," she murmured.

"You a good girl, huh?"

Kirby shrugged. "I guess so."

"Shit, they say good girls are just bad girls that never got caught..." Castle passed the blunt to Kirby again in hopes that she would hit it. He hated a square bitch.

Surprisingly, Kirby grabbed it and took a light pull. A flurry of hoarse coughs came soon after. She felt like she'd hacked up an organ. She had never smoked a day in her life. Wheezing and hacking, Kirby quickly passed the L back to Castle.

He took a couple tokes before lowering his window. "You good?"

"Yes," Kirby struggled to say.

"So what's ya name, Virgin Lungs?"

She laughed a little. "Kirby. And yours?"

"Castle Maurice Black III."

Kirby loved how regal his name sounded. It fit him so well. "Is that your real name?" she asked.

Castle laughed and it warmed her heart. She noticed that he now had a gold bottom grill in.

The single piece of jewelry alone cost more than her home was worth. "Baby girl, I'm too old for aliases and nicknames, and shit."

"What's too old?" Kirby asked curiously.

"A whole lot older than you, youngin'."

"How old?" she pressed.

"Guess."

"*Hmm*." Kirby rested an index finger on her right cheek's dimple. "I'mma say... Thirty maybe...."

Castle nodded his head appreciatively. Her irrepressible innocence and naivety captivated him. She was young enough to be molded and groomed. That was the main reason he loved young hoes. "Close," he said. "Thirty-six."

"Oh."

Castle didn't miss the flatness in her tone. "What'chu mean 'oh'?" he chuckled. "That too old for you?"

Kirby paused. Castle made her nervous. She barely knew anything about him, but she was sure she'd never met anyone like him. There was an enigmatic aura that surrounded him; he had a boss-like presence. She envisioned him as a man in charge, but she had no idea to what extent. She might've fled if she knew he was top dog of a multi-million dollar drug operation.

"I'm not sure. I never dated anyone in their thirties."

"Do you date at all," was Castle's next question.

"...Not really," Kirby answered, slightly embarrassed. She thought about lying but it was what it was. The boys at her school weren't really checking for her, and the few who did were never taken seriously. Either that, or they just weren't her type.

"So you mean to tell me yo' ass never had a boyfriend before?" he asked. "You ain't gotta lie to me, baby girl. One thing about me, I hate a fuckin' liar—"

"I'm not lying," she promised.

"You ever fucked before?"

Kirby's cheeks flushed in embarrassment. She wasn't expecting such a bold question. "No," she squeaked out.

"You ain't ever fucked before. You ain't ever had a boyfriend before. Why do I find that shit so hard to believe? How come you never had a boyfriend?"

Kirby shrugged. "I don't know. No one's really grabbed my interest, I guess."

"That's 'cuz you ain't ever fucked with a real nigga."

Castle slowly eased his car in front of Kirby's house. The building he pulled in front of hardly looked livable, but it was the destination his navigational system had led him to.

Kirby took her time unfastening her seatbelt. "Where you from, if you don't mind me asking. You mentioned you weren't from around here...and you have an accent."

"Oh yeah?" Castle chuckled, and his grill sparkled. "I'm from Atlanta, baby. Born and raised."

"That's cool. I hear a lot about Atlanta. What's it like?"

"Like Black Hollywood."

It sounded like somewhere she'd like to one-day visit. Lingering on the doorknob, Kirby almost didn't want to leave, but she knew her mother was waiting on her. As her health gradually degenerated, she had become increasingly immobile. Kirby couldn't leave her alone for extended periods.

"Shit, take my number though," he told her. "I'm only in town for a couple days, then I'm headed to Vegas. You ever been?"

"I never even left Philadelphia."

"Real shit? Damn. That's all bad. Fuck with me then. We could fly out together. It's fight weekend so shit's gon' be crazy."

"Fight weekend? What's that?"

Castle looked over at Kirby in disbelief. "You don't get out much, do you? Just a small city girl that ain't 'een stepped foot in the real world."

Kirby shrugged. She didn't have a comeback.

"Floyd and Pacquiao fightin' at the MGM."

"Who are they?"

Castle chuckled. "Boxers. Damn, baby. You live under a rock? You must not be into social media."

"Not really. Between work and school I barely have time to keep up with entertainment."

Castle loved that she wasn't big on social media. "I dig that. And ain't nothin' to be sorry about," he said. "You handlin' ya business. I like that shit. I can respect it. But yeah, like I was sayin', it's gon' be dope. I'm tryin' to brush shoulders with stars. You should fuck with a nigga. I'd show you a good time." He tried to gauge her interest with talk of celebrities.

"I can't just up and leave. I have to take care of my mama. She can't stay alone for long periods of time."

"Why? What's wrong with her?"

"She's...sick." Kirby wasn't ready to tell him that Leah was dying of cancer.

"Lemme handle that fuh you then," he offered.

"How?"

Castle shrugged like it was no big deal. "Shit, I'll pay somebody to do that."

Kirby laughed as if he'd said a joke. When she realized he was dead serious, she stopped and stared at him. She then thought about the crisp hundred-dollar tip he'd left her at the pub. "You really are for real, ain't you?"

"Do I look like a nigga that play games?" Castle took her hand in his, gently caressing her knuckles. His hands were large, rough and calloused in comparison to her smaller, softer ones. Years of prison, slinging, and gun toting had hardened him.

"No. But what about school?" Kirby asked. "I still have a couple weeks left 'til graduation—"

"Couple weeks?" he scoffed. "That's it? Well, shit, I guess we'll get up next time then. Gon' 'head and finish up ya'll lil' school year. There may be other opportunities."

Kirby didn't like the way that sounded. Castle made it seem as if she might not see him again after that day, and she wasn't feeling that.

"What if I *did* wanna go though," Kirby suddenly said. "We barely know each other...shouldn't we get to know each other first? I mean I never did this before..."

Castle could see that she was toying with the idea. Young and naïve, she couldn't help being gullible. Kirby was pure like raw cocaine—and just as lethal. Castle knew the consequences for fucking with an underage girl, but he still wanted her.

She had one of two choices. She could take the blue pill and return to her boring, everyday life while struggling to make ends meet. Or...she could take the red pill and allow Castle to make a woman out of her young ass.

"We can get to know each other on this lil' trip." Castle reached over and trailed his fingertip along her thigh. He had a solution for every excuse she hit him with. Kirby had actually run out of them altogether.

"I...I still don't know," she hesitated. "I...Maybe I need time to think about it."

"I'm leaving Thursday. So don't take too long to think about it, aight."

"I won't..." Kirby could feel things heating up between them. She'd never felt so much intensity with a guy before. "I'll call you," she said, opening the passenger door

"I'll be waitin'," he smiled. Castle enjoyed a good cat-and-mouse game, just as long as the other person made it worthwhile. He could smell that tight, illicitly sweet pussy from his seat. There was no pussy better than virgin pussy.

She bullshitting right now, but she'll be mine in no time, Castle told himself. He'd make sure of that.

Kirby carefully climbed out and headed towards her house. As she ascended the cracked stone steps, she could feel Castle's dark eyes penetrating her. If she could've saw into the future, she would've ran without looking back. She would've never climbed in his shiny Rolls Royce...and she certainly wouldn't have called him.

It was an inauspicious beginning to a long and complex relationship.

UP NEXT! TEXT BOOKS TO 25827 TO BE NOTIFIED WHEN IT DROPS!

JADED PUBLICATIONS PRESENTS

HONOR My Gangsta

PEBBLES STARR

JADED PUBLICATIONS Presents

Beauty
And
The Boss

PEBBLES STARR

Made in the USA
San Bernardino, CA
19 February 2017